"Whe

Cindy asked.

"You should ask your mother that question," Jenny replied.

"My mommy died when I was little."

"My mother died when I was a little girl, too," Jenny told her, joining Cindy on the front porch step.

"Do you still get sad sometimes?"

"Sometimes."

"Me, too. I'm glad you moved here. You're gonna like my daddy. All girls like my daddy. He's a poplar man. More poplar than the Beast!"

Just what she needed, Jenny thought to herself. A little girl with heartbreak eyes and a man with the popularity of a beast....

Dear Reader,

This month, wedding bells ring for six couples who marry for convenient reasons—and discover love by surprise. Join us for their HASTY WEDDINGS.

Kasey Michaels starts off the month with *Timely Matrimony*, a love story with a time-travel twist. It's all in the timing for modern-day bride Suzi Harper, and Harry Wilde, her handsome husband from the nineteenth century. Just as they found happiness, it seemed Harry's destiny was to leave her....

In Anne Peters's *McCullough's Bride*, handsome rancher Nick McCullough rescues single mom Beth Coleman the only way he knows how—he marries her! Now Nick is the one in danger—of losing his heart to a woman who could never return his love.

Popular Desire author Cathie Linz weaves a *One of a Kind Marriage*. In this fast-paced romp, Jenny Benjamin and Rafe Murphy start as enemies, then become man and wife. Marriage may have solved their problems, but can love cure their differences?

The impromptu nuptials continue with *Oh, Baby!*, Lauryn Chandler's humorous look at a single woman who is determined to have a child—and lands herself a husband in the bargain. It's a green card marriage for Kelsey Shepherd and Frankie Falco in *Temporary Groom*. Jayne Addison continues her Falco Family series with this story of short-term commitment—and unending attraction! The laughter continues with Carolyn Zane's *Wife in Name Only*—a tale of marriage—under false pretenses.

I hope you enjoy our HASTY WEDDINGS. In the coming months, look for more books by your favorite authors.

Happy reading,

Anne Canadeo
Senior Editor

Please address questions and book requests to:
Silhouette Reader Service
U.S.: 3010 Walden Ave., P.O. Box 1325, Buffalo, NY 14269
Canadian: P.O. Box 609, Fort Erie, Ont. L2A 5X3

ONE OF A KIND MARRIAGE

Cathie Linz

Silhouette
R O M A N C E™
Published by Silhouette Books
America's Publisher of Contemporary Romance

Many thanks to Teddy Bear BB
and the talented teddy-bear artists,
with special thanks to Phyllis and Kay.

This book is dedicated to Sarah Galanter,
who began as a reader and ended up a friend,
saving me whenever I got "farzorked"—thanks, Cappy!

 SILHOUETTE BOOKS

ISBN 0-373-19032-8

ONE OF A KIND MARRIAGE

Copyright © 1994 by Cathie L. Baumgardner

Printed in U.S.A.

Books by Cathie Linz

Silhouette Romance

One of a Kind Marriage #1032

Silhouette Desire

Change of Heart #408
A Friend in Need #443
As Good as Gold #484
Adam's Way #519
Smiles #575
Handyman #616
Smooth Sailing #665
Flirting with Trouble #722
Male Ordered Bride #761
Escapades #804
Midnight Ice #846

CATHIE LINZ

was in her mid-twenties when she left her career in a university law library to become a full-time writer of contemporary romance fiction. Since then, this best-selling Chicago author has had over twenty books published. She recently won the *Romantic Times* Career Achievement Award for Best Storyteller of the Year.

An avid world traveler, Cathie often uses humorous mishaps from her own trips as inspiration for her stories. Such was the case with this book, inspired by a trip to New England in the fall. In addition, Cathie's research from a previous book—*As Good as Gold*—led her into the captivating world of teddy-bear artists.

After traveling, Cathie is always glad to get back home to her two cats, her new collection of teddy bears, her trusty word processor and her chache of Oreo cookies!

DESIGN FOR:
BENJAMIN BEAR
WEDDING

Chapter One

"Where do babies come from?" Jenny Benjamin's five-year-old neighbor, Cindy asked her. She'd been tagging after Jenny, asking unstoppable and frequently unanswerable questions, since Jenny had started moving into her new—albeit rather old—home this morning. After almost a month of tying up the details surrounding the sale, Jenny was finally going to be sleeping in her own place tonight, instead of staying with her friend Miriam.

Although she'd only been in North Dunway, New Hampshire for a few weeks, Jenny had managed to make a lot of new friends in that time—the youngest and most persistent of them being little Cindy from next door. Every time Jenny came outside to bring in another box of belongings, Cindy was right there waiting for her. The little girl was adorable with her short, curly brown hair and big brown eyes. But her questioning tactics put the Spanish Inquisition to shame.

"You should ask your mother that question," Jenny replied.

"My mommy died when I was little," Cindy said. "But I'm a big girl now and hardly miss her all the time anymores."

"My mother died when I was a little girl, too," Jenny told her, sitting down to join Cindy on the front porch step.

Cindy turned to look at her, staring at her with eyes that were painfully candid. "Yeah?"

"Yeah."

"Do you still get sad sometimes 'bout it?" Cindy asked.

Jenny nodded. "Sometimes."

"Me, too. I'm glad you moved here. You can be my friend if you want," Cindy declared.

"I'd like that, Cindy. I'd like that a lot."

"You're gonna like my daddy," Cindy added. "All girls like my daddy. He's a poplar man. More poplar than The Beast!"

Just what she needed, Jenny thought to herself. A little girl with heartbreak eyes and a man with the popularity of a beast. Sounded like a distracting combination.

But Jenny hadn't come here to North Dunway for distractions. She'd come to work and she'd couldn't afford to forget that fact. Too much was riding on her succeeding here. While it was true that her grandmother had bequeathed a sizable sum of money to Jenny in her will, it was for a "dowry" and it wasn't accessible until she got married—a move not in Jenny's immediate game plans.

No, Jenny was financially on her own here. This move was a double-or-nothing roll of the dice for her.

Jenny only hoped that her luck would continue to hold and that everything would work out in the end. Until then, she had to cope with Cindy's latest question. "So where *do* babies come from?"

"Perfect!" Jenny exclaimed as she sat back from her work table several nights later to gaze at her latest creation—Bonita Bear. "Your ears were too small—that's where

I went wrong. You look *much* better now." Jenny paused to affectionately pat Bonita's embroidered nose. "Don't you agree, guys?" Jenny asked the assembly of various-size teddy bears sitting in a semicircle around her worktable. "She's perfect, right? Just like the rest of you."

As an award-winning teddy-bear artist, Jenny always surrounded herself with her creations when she was working. They provided her with inspiration. They also provided her with her livelihood, for what had started out as a hobby had grown into a booming mail-order business.

It had begun almost four years ago when Benjamin Bear, her first successful design, had won several Best of Show awards at teddy-bear conventions around the country as well as a coveted Golden Teddy Award. Since that time several other bears had followed: Bertram, a fuzzy little guy with a mischievous expression; Grandfather Bear, a throwback to early teddy bears with his wool-tweed body and shoe button eyes. Then there was also an ongoing series of baby Bambino Bears, each one unique. Jenny loved them all. And so did the public, if recent sales figures were any gauge.

In fact, Jenny could hardly keep up with all the orders pouring in, which was why she'd taken the plunge and relocated from the cramped quarters of her two bedroom apartment in Connecticut to this place—located on the western edge of the tourist town of North Dunway, New Hampshire. With a main road out front and wooded hills behind, the property had a very comfy feeling. Not too far out for Jenny to feel isolated yet not set smack dab in the crowded center of town so she'd feel hemmed in. Like Goldilocks, this place fit her just right. In fact, she had the best of both worlds as the wooded hillsides at the back of the property gave it a country feel while she was in reality only a five minute drive from the center of town.

At one time, probably a hundred and fifty years ago, her property had been part of a farm, but now the only remaining farm building was the barn. Actually Jenny had bought the property more for the barn out back than for the house. The barn, with its spacious interior, was the perfect site for the rapidly expanding Benjamin Bear and Company.

For the moment, the office where she sat was the only even partially usable space, but renovation work was already underway, and in another two weeks the place would be finished. Or so the contractor, Mr. Gardner, assured her. She hoped he was right.

It looked like everything was finally coming together, including the design for Bonita Bear.

"I think I've finally found the perfect partner for you, Benjamin." Jenny set the newly restyled prototype Bonita right next to Benjamin Bear. "There." Jenny tilted her head to one side and studied the pair for a moment before nodding approvingly. "You guys look like you were made for each other. What do you think of her, Benjamin? Pretty cute, huh?" She grinned. "You know, it's a good thing it's two in the morning and there's no one else around because some people might think I was a little strange talking to teddy bears. Of course, no self-respecting bear fan would have a problem with it, but others might. But, hey, what do we care, right?" She sat Bonita Bear up a little straighter and then frowned. "I wonder if your ears are *too* big now?"

At that moment Jenny's own ears detected a noise from outside the barn. At first she shrugged it off as the nighttime ramblings of a friendly pair of raccoons she'd been feeding behind the barn. But then the noise got louder, closer, and more recognizable. It was the sound of footsteps—human footsteps!

Jenny suddenly became aware of the fact that she was in a very vulnerable position—alone in an empty barn in the middle of the night. The shadowy interior of the barn took on sinister overtones. Acting on instinct, she grabbed the first large thing that came to hand. Only after the fact did she realize that it was a four-foot-high teddy bear.

Out of the darkness came the sound of a mocking masculine voice. "What are you planning on doing with that thing?" he drawled. "Have it hug me to death?"

"Stay away from me!" she warned the intruder in a forceful voice, wielding the bear in a threatening way.

"Now, is that any way to greet a neighbor?" The man stepped into the pool of light. "I'm Rafe Murphy. Cindy's dad. We met when you first moved in. I live next door, remember?"

Jenny remembered him, all right. Who wouldn't? Tall, dark and brooding, Rafe Murphy was a very memorable man. With his bad-boy eyes and chiseled mouth, he was the kind of man your mother warned you against—the kind that made you want to say yes when you knew you should say no. Even in the barn's dim light she could see that certain knowing look in his blue eyes, which were several shades darker than her own.

Seeing his amused look at the oversize bear she still held in her hands, Jenny hastily set it on her chair before asking in concern, "Is Cindy all right? Is something wrong?"

"Cindy is fine."

"Then what are you doing here at this time of night?" she demanded. She knew Rafe was Cindy's dad and that he owned Murphy's, the restaurant next door to her property, but that didn't explain what he was doing in her barn in the middle of the night. Or why he'd snuck up on her the way he had, scaring her half to death. "Don't tell me you've come to borrow a cup of sugar?"

"No. I came to talk to you. I was closing my place up for the night and I saw your lights on over here. You don't usually work this late."

How did he know that? Jenny wondered suspiciously. The possibility that he might be keeping tabs on her disturbed her. *He* disturbed her. There was something more than just slightly untamed about the man. Wearing a black sweater and slacks, he had the lean build and devil-may-care confidence of a cat burglar.

"How did you get in?" she asked distrustfully. "I locked the door."

"It was open when I got here."

Jenny could have sworn she'd locked the door, but she wasn't about to stand there arguing with him at this late hour. "You still haven't told me why you're here," she reminded him.

"I told you, I want to talk to you."

"At this time of the night? About what? You know I really don't appreciate you slipping in here and scaring me the way you did." She hadn't appreciated the silent way he'd laughed at her, either!

"The next time you get scared, pick up the phone instead of a stupid stuffed toy," Rafe curtly advised her. "That thing wouldn't have given you much protection if I really *had* been an intruder."

His tone of voice did not improve her mood any. "Thank you so much for that security lesson. Tell me something, Mr. Murphy. Are all the other neighbors as good at scaring people as you are, or is this your own personal specialty?"

Instead of answering, Rafe just stood there and studied her. She had her hands propped on her hips and was glaring at him with exasperated belligerence. Her shoulder-length light brown hair was parted on the side and fell over her forehead, just shy of her big sky-blue eyes. Her lips were made for kissing, her creamy skin made for touching.

Reminding himself that he was here for a reason, a *business* reason, Rafe looked away from Jenny. Shifting his attention to the empty office behind her, he said, "I thought I heard you talking to someone in here."

"I was just talking to myself."

He raised an eyebrow. "Do that often, do you?"

"Occasionally. But I'm sure you didn't mosey over here at two in the morning to discuss my personal quirks."

"I don't know." Rafe couldn't stop himself from studying her lips. They were curvy and soft. So was she. "Your personal quirks might be very interesting," he murmured softly.

Jenny shifted nervously. His smoky blue eyes were conveying messages that were strictly male-to-female. "Thanks for your concern, but there's no need for you to worry. As you can see, I'm fine. You may leave now."

"Oh, I may, may I?" His eyes abruptly iced over. "Nobody gives me orders, lady."

Jenny's eyes narrowed. "Ah, at last…something we have in common. No one gives me orders, either, Mr. Murphy. Remember that and we'll get along just fine."

"I hear you've been talking to my daughter, Cindy," Rafe declared.

"That's right. Is there a law against that?"

"She's only five."

"And?"

"She gets hurt easily."

"You came over here at two in the morning to warn me against hurting your daughter?" Jenny said in disbelief.

"No, I came over to make you a proposition."

Jenny's disbelief quickly turned to wariness. "What kind of proposition?"

"Suspicious little thing, aren't you?"

Jenny straightened her shoulders, adding another quarter inch to her not insignificant five-foot-seven height. "Another thing you should know about me, Mr. Murphy, is that I don't like being called little."

"You think we can have a civil conversation here without you flying off the handle?" Rafe inquired with a masculine condescension that Jenny found infuriating.

"I'm sure we can, providing you stop putting your foot in your mouth," she sweetly retorted.

"You've got this princess act down pat, don't you?" Rafe noted. "The frosty tone of voice, the regal look."

"Regal look? Really?" Jenny had to smile at the absurdity. "Since when have a flannel shirt and jeans been considered royal attire?"

"Depends who's wearing them," Rafe retorted. He could only guess at the curves hidden by her loose-fitting shirt, but the way she was wearing those jeans was definitely affecting him. So was her voice, a husky combination of fire and ice. Too bad she was so temperamental and haughty. Rafe preferred women who were quiet and shy—the way Susan had been. At the memory of his dead wife, bittersweet pain pierced its way straight through him.

It had been four years since Susan had died. Rafe liked to think he'd come to terms with his emotions and with her death after a yearlong battle with cancer. It was time to get on with his life. Some days it was easier to do that than others.

Seeing the shadowy twists of pain in Rafe's eyes, Jenny softly asked, "Is something wrong?"

At her question, an invisible wall came down, shielding his emotions from her view. Most of them, anyway. A generous dash of impatience was still very much in evidence as he replied, "Yes, something is wrong. You've been ignoring my calls, that's what's wrong. I've phoned several times over the past few days and left messages on that dumb machine of yours," he said. "Why haven't you returned my calls?"

"I've been very busy." The truth was that Cindy's sexy and very "poplar" dad made Jenny very nervous. And that was *before* she'd even spent any time with him. Now that Jenny was face-to-face with him, she was even more jumpy. She was also annoyed by his domineering attitude. She didn't like him treating her as some kind of anomaly that he by turns either found amusing or irritating.

"You're telling me you were too busy to pick up a phone for a minute?" Rafe demanded. "I was calling you concerning a business matter."

"What business, Mr. Murphy?"

"The name is Rafe. And the business concerns this property. As you've no doubt discovered by now, the place is pretty run-down. Old Man Miller let it go to sh—go down the toilet," he substituted. "I'm willing to make you a generous offer to buy the place from you."

"You must be kidding! I just moved in. I'm not about to turn around and move out again."

"You haven't even heard my offer yet."

"It doesn't matter. I'm not interested in selling, whatever your offer is."

"I'm talking about a very generous price," Rafe stated.

"I don't care," Jenny firmly declared. She'd made the decision to move here, and spent a great deal of money getting the place ready. She had new catalogs all printed up with her new address. "I'm not moving. I've got a business to run here."

"What kind of business are you going to run out of a barn?"

"A profitable one," was all Jenny said before asking a question of her own. "How long have you been in the restaurant business?"

Her change of subject made him frown. "Seven years. Why?"

"That long?" Jenny shook her head. "I'm amazed you've been able to stay in business that long considering your anti-social attitude."

"That your way of telling me that I've been rude?" he inquired.

"Bingo! You've obviously got a chip on your shoulder the size of Mount Washington and I'd like to know why," Jenny bluntly said.

"Let's just say we come from *very* different worlds."

"You don't have the faintest idea what kind of world I come from," Jenny pointed out. "We haven't exchanged more than a dozen words since I moved in at the beginning of the month. Luckily your daughter is much more talkative than you are."

"Meaning what?"

"Meaning I know you're from Chicago originally. Your dad, a retired navy man, lives with you and helps take care of Cindy. The three of you live above the restaurant. Oh, and apparently your dad has a tattoo of a naked woman on his right arm."

"My daughter, the blabbermouth," Rafe noted with equal parts of exasperation and displeasure.

"Whereas you prefer not to give out anything more than name, rank and serial number."

"My dad is the one who was in the service, not me. How did we get started on this subject, anyway?"

"I turned down your offer to buy me out and you started hurling insults."

"Talk about exaggerating things entirely out of proportion...." Rafe said.

"It's two in the morning, Rafe," she interrupted him to say. "I don't want to continue this argument any longer than necessary. It's been a long day."

"For me, too."

"Another thing we have in common then. We're both successful business people who are self-employed and put in long hours. It just so happens that you're in the restaurant business and I'm in the manufacturing business."

"What do you manufacture?"

"Teddy bears," Jenny replied.

"You're kidding, right?"

She shook her head. "Not at all."

"Cindy said something about you having a lot of teddy bears, but...what kind of business is making teddy bears?"

"As I said before, it's a very profitable business," she replied.

"I can't believe you're refusing to sell this property to me because you're going to stay here and make something so—"

"You've already put your foot in your mouth at least twice this evening," Jenny inserted with a narrow-eyed look that was very clear in its message. "I'd be very careful of doing it a third time."

"You actually make things like that?" he asked, pointing to the oversize teddy bear she'd almost whacked him over the head with.

"No, that's a commercial bear. Those are mine." She pointed to the group assembled on her worktable.

As Rafe moved closer, it occurred to Jenny that lingering in an empty barn with him wasn't the brightest idea she'd ever had. He was rude and too sexy for his own good. Or hers for that matter.

"Be careful what you say," she warned him as he gave her bears what she considered to be a disparaging look. "If you think I flew off the handle before, that's nothing compared to what I'll say if you insult my work."

"They look okay," he finally said.

"Gee, thanks." Talk about damning with faint praise, she thought to herself. Why did he seem to find it so hard to be encouraging...? Wrong choice of word, Jenny immediately corrected herself, remembering the heated flare she'd seen in his eyes earlier. She certainly didn't want him encouraging her.

Rafe turned to face her. "So you plan on staying here and manufacturing teddy bears?"

"That's right."

"Here, in the barn?"

"Right again." She waved a hand at the sawdust covered floors and half-completed walls. "It may not look like much now, but when the construction is done, you won't recognize the place."

"Why this particular barn?"

"It has the space I need and I could afford it."

"There are plenty of other places you could afford with just as much space. In fact, you could afford even more space if you'd accept my offer. As I said before, I'm not hurting for money. I'm willing to pay you twice what you paid for this property."

"Why do you want it so much?"

"Because I plan on expanding my restaurant."

Jenny had only seen Rafe's Victorian mansion-turned-restaurant from the outside, but she'd heard via word of mouth that the food served inside was delicious. Obviously the place was popular and successful. Expansion was a logical step. "So, what's stopping you?"

"You are. The new addition would be in this direction. There's no room for expansion on the other three sides of my property."

"Then why didn't you buy this property when it first came on the market?"

"I tried. In fact, I thought I'd succeeded. Old man Miller and I had an agreement. Then you showed up."

"You'd signed a purchase contract with him?" Jenny asked, surprised by this news.

"No," Rafe had to admit, "but we were on the verge of doing so. Then you showed up."

"And I promised not to tear down this barn, which has been in Mr. Miller's family for generations. With that in mind, he decided to sell his house and barn to me. Which he had every right to do. He may have been a bit strange, but the choice of buyer was his to make."

"Why do you want to stay here?" Rafe demanded, making no attempt to hide his irritation from her. "Your business could be located anywhere."

"I like it here," she said simply.

Her reply seemed to anger him even further. "That's not a logical reason!"

"It is to me." She shrugged, unable to resist feeling an element of satisfaction at having irritated him half as much as he'd irritated her.

"Then you won't sell?"

"That's what I've been saying for the past fifteen minutes. I'm not selling." When Rafe looked as if he were actually going to grind his teeth in frustration, she took pity on him and said, "Can't you add on to your restaurant out the back?"

"There isn't enough room for the banquet facilities I want to add."

"I'm sorry."

"Don't be sorry," Rafe shot back. "It's not over yet. You might still change your mind and decide to sell. You haven't been here very long. You might find that you don't like the place as much as you thought you would."

"That sounds rather ominous," she noted.

"Reality often is."

"This isn't a passing whim, Mr. Murphy. I've thought about this move very carefully."

"As carefully as you thought about picking up that stupid bear to attack an intruder with?" he inquired mockingly. "Being in charge of your own business requires clearer thinking than that. Doesn't bode well for your future success."

Her look was laced with sarcasm and anger. So was her voice. "Of course, I should have known that a man with your many talents would have the ability to forecast the future, as well. Can you also tell me who's going to win the Super Bowl this year? Or how about the World Series? The lottery?"

"It doesn't take much brains to predict that you're not going to stick to this very long."

"Only someone with no brains at all would make such a stupid prediction based on nothing but their own petty resentment that I won't do things their way!"

"Now who's being rude?" he countered.

"Your bad habits must be wearing off on me," she shot back. "In any case, it's much too late to be standing here arguing with you."

Rafe noted that Jenny had her hands on her hips again, drawing his attention to their soft curves. Rafe grinned as the title of one of his favorite fifties tunes came to his mind. "Venus in Blue Jeans." Yeah, that image fit her better than princess did. She looked like a Venus in Blue Jeans.

There was more than one way to skin a cat, and more than one way to get a woman to change her mind, Rafe decided.

"If you're ready to lock up, I'll walk you over to your house," he told her.

"That isn't necessary."

"Yeah, I know. I'm just being chivalrous. Enjoy it while you can. It's only a temporary condition."

"In that case..." She picked up a few of her bears and handed them to him. "You can help me carry the gang back to the house."

"Why not leave them here?"

"Because—" she smiled at the sight of tough-guy Rafe Murphy standing there gingerly holding an armful of bears as if they were dynamite "—they'd get lonely out here." She perched Benjamin Bear on one hip and carried Bonita in her other hand. At eighteen inches high, they were both an armful. "I couldn't leave them all by themselves in the dark."

"Of course you couldn't," Rafe said mockingly. "You sound like Cindy."

"She looks a lot like you."

"She looks even more like her mother."

"I'm sorry about your wife...." Jenny trailed off, not knowing quite how to express her sympathy.

He made no reply and something about his attitude warned Jenny not to press him on the subject.

It was a warning she heeded, but it left her at a loss for something to say. She noticed he was no longer wearing a wedding ring, but clearly he was still recovering from his wife's death, which no doubt accounted for his dark and brooding demeanor. The silence was strained as they left the barn. Jenny had just locked the barn's side door when she heard a noise.

Startled, she whirled around and gasped. "What was that?"

A second later a mama raccoon and three little roly-poly babies waddled past a moonlit patch of ground. The sight of them made Jenny smile. "Oh, look. It's just the raccoons. Aren't they cute?"

"No. They're a nuisance." Rafe turned to give her a disapproving look. "I hope you're not feeding them."

"Why not?"

"Because they're wild animals and need to fend for themselves. You're not doing them any favors."

"Everyone needs a little help now and again," she said quietly. "Even raccoons."

"They're just scavengers. They're not lapdogs."

"I'm not partial to lapdogs."

"Prefer wild animals, do you?" he inquired.

They both knew they were no longer discussing the local wildlife here. "So long as they don't bite the hand that feeds them," she replied.

"Animals have a habit of doing that."

By now they'd reached the rickety back steps of the farmhouse. Rafe frowned at their precarious state of disrepair. "You really should get these fixed. It's a miracle you haven't broken your neck."

"That would be one way for you to get this property, wouldn't it?" Jenny didn't know what made her say that; it just sort of slipped out.

Rafe was not amused. He shoved the bears at her with a disregard for their well-being that made her cry out in protest. "Hey, be careful with those!" she exclaimed.

"You stay out here any longer and *you're* the one who's going to have to be careful. I've just about reached the end of my patience with you," he warned her.

"No kidding," she muttered. Obviously Rafe's dark looks were matched by dark moods. Her earlier statement may have been careless but there was no reason for him to overreact this way.

"Keep my offer in mind," he advised her curtly. "And get those stairs fixed." A moment later he was gone, blending back into the darkness with the ease of one who was accustomed to prowling in the night.

"So much for the wild animals of North Dunway," Jenny murmured. "That one definitely bites."

Her words carried in the darkness to Rafe, who was standing several yards away, waiting to make sure she got safely inside.

The only warning she had of his presence was a sudden gleam in the darkness. His grin was a wolfish slash of white.

"Oh, I bite all right," he murmured, just loud enough for her to hear him. "But not until I know you better."

The sound of his soft laughter followed Jenny up the stairs as she hurried into the house, slamming the door behind her with a force that startled the local wildlife and delighted Rafe.

"And I will get to know you better," he promised her and himself. "Much better. You can count on it."

Chapter Two

Jenny did not sleep well that night and woke the next morning with vague memories of vivid dreams centered around a wolf—a wolf with Rafe Murphy's slashing grin and bad-boy eyes. She found herself humming "Who's Afraid of the Big Bad Wolf?" while taking her shower and getting dressed in a cotton knit skirt along with a matching light blue sweater that was long enough to cup her bottom.

"Too many late nights," she admonished her reflection in the mirror as she applied her light makeup. "Talking to teddy bears is fine, dreaming about Rafe Murphy is not." She closed her eyeshadow case with a decided snap. "So don't go getting any ideas. You know you have bad luck where men are concerned," she sternly reminded herself. "Besides, you've got enough problems getting Benjamin Bear and Company started. You don't need any more trouble. Remember that."

Her self-lecture and her makeup application completed, she headed for the kitchen, rubbing her arms as she did so. It was cool in the house as she'd turned the thermostat down last night. Looked like their bout of Indian summer was coming to an end, she noted with a tiny shiver. Autumn was definitely here, and in this part of New Hampshire winter wouldn't be far behind. A bowl of hot cereal would be the perfect beginning for a crisp October day like this one.

As she waited for the cereal to cook on the somewhat temperamental old gas stove, the phone rang. She picked up the kitchen extension. "Hello?"

"Leave," a muffled male voice said.

"You must have the wrong number." She hung up. Teenagers with their dumb crank calls. Rafe might want her off her property, but he was a respected member of North Dunway's business community. He wouldn't resort to a crank call like that. He'd face her directly and try and wheel and deal his way over her property line. Not that he'd get very far.

Dismissing the call from her mind, Jenny absently ran her fingertips over the soft texture of her sweater. It was one of her favorites, not only for the lovely blue color but for the smooth weave of the cotton material.

Jenny had always been a very tactile person, into "feelies" as her grandmother had called it—appreciating things like the richness of sandwashed silk, the inviting smoothness of fine cotton, the nap of supple suede. Growing up, her clothing had mostly been secondhand castaways which her grandmother, a wonderful seamstress, had taken in or let out to fit her. It had only been recently that Jenny had been able to indulge in and savor the pleasure of having her favorite textures against her skin, including not only her clothing but also the two-hundred-and-fifty thread count cotton sheets covering her bed and the thick towels in her bathroom.

Her appreciation of tactile things was also reflected in her choice of materials for her bears. As she ate her breakfast she thumbed through a sampler of materials that a supplier had just sent her—fine imported mohairs and butter-soft plushes.

Jenny was just pouring her second mug full of coffee when there was a knock at the back door. "Is that caffeine I smell?" her assistant and friend, Miriam Weiss, demanded as she let herself in.

"Help yourself," Jenny invited with a grin. Miriam was the reason Jenny had ended up in New Hampshire. The two had met in New York City at a bear convention—Jenny had to pause a moment to think back—goodness, it must be five years ago now. They'd gotten on instantly and had forged a friendship that only got stronger over time; Miriam's directness and mocking humor being the perfect compliment to Jenny's more reserved nature.

When Miriam and her husband, Max, had moved up here to New Hampshire last year, Miriam had hounded Jenny about moving out of her small rented apartment in Connecticut; dropping hints like carrots, talking about what a great place for the creative arts this area around the White Mountains was, until in the end Jenny had come up for a visit and fallen in love with the area. Within a week, she'd put money down on her present place. The rest, as they say, was history.

"I see the workmen are busy sprucing up the barn," Miriam said as she poured herself a cup of coffee.

"They are?" This was news to Jenny, who had yet to see any workmen appear on the job so far that morning.

"I was being sarcastic," Miriam retorted. "It's nine and there isn't a workman in sight."

"Mr. Gardner assured me that he'd have his best crew here a little later this morning."

"And they get here a little *later* every morning," Miriam muttered before taking a sip of coffee. "That's the problem."

"He claims he's back on schedule with the construction...."

"*Claim* being the operative word there," Miriam added. "I've told you, you've got to ride herd on those *schlemiels.*"

Jenny had to smile at the older woman's scolding tone and language. "You mean the same way I ride herd on you?"

"Herd-schmerd! Hah! You never ride herd on me. Lucky for you I'm just naturally a hard worker. The same can't be said for everyone."

"I'll keep an eye on the workmen, and if they aren't on the job by ten, I'll call Mr. Gardner and give him what-for. How's that sound?"

"Better."

"Good." Picking up her teddy-bear-decorated mug of coffee, Jenny headed for the large dining room that was temporarily being used as an office. Two computers were in the room, as well as a fax machine, a copier and boxes of supplies. Since the workmen were scheduled to finish the inside walls in the barn that week, Jenny wouldn't be using the office space out there again until the work was completed. Besides, she didn't want her sexy neighbor making any more unscheduled after-midnight visits. "Did you track down that shipment of joint sets yet?" Jenny asked Miriam.

"The supplier says they shipped them two weeks ago. They're going to send out a replacement shipment."

"Good. We can't go into production without those parts. And did you take care of the paperwork for the new employees?"

Miriam nodded. "All taken care of."

"Great." With the five new employees, Jenny would soon be the proud employer of six—a manageable number for her cottage industry. Only three of the five would actually be working in the barn studio, the other two were mothers with small children who would be doing handwork in their own homes. Jenny's own mother had been forced to go out to work in order to support them, so she was glad to be able to help these mothers stay home with their children during those critical early years. "How about those orders—" Jenny was interrupted by a knock at the front door.

"You expecting anyone?" Miriam asked.

Jenny shook her head. "Maybe it's the deliveryman with that missing shipment."

"No, it's not the deliveryman," Miriam replied, leaning forward in her chair enough to look through the frosted glass that comprised the top two thirds of the front door. "Not unless he's shrunk since the last time I saw him."

Jenny opened her front door to find Cindy standing there. And in her arms the little girl held one of the most bedraggled-looking teddy bears Jenny had ever seen.

"Bruiser needs fixing," Cindy breathlessly told Jenny. "His insides are coming out."

"I can see that."

"Grandpa was gonna throw him away but I saved him. Can you make Bruiser all better?"

"Well, I suppose I can try." Although it wasn't her main focus, Jenny had read a number of books on how to repair bears. She'd even saved a few bears from the dustbin herself.

"Good." Carefully shifting Bruiser to one arm, Cindy used her other hand to reach into her jeans pocket and take out a handful of change. "This is all the money I got right now." She opened her hand to display the few coins she held in her palm. "Will it be 'nuf to fix Bruiser?"

"I don't need your money, Cindy." Jenny gently closed her hand around the little girl's much-smaller hand and nudged it back toward the pocket from where the money had come. "You keep it."

"And who have we here?" Miriam asked, joining Jenny at the front door.

"Bruiser," the little girl replied. "An' I'm Cindy."

"Is that your bear?" Miriam asked.

Cindy shook her head. "It used to be daddy's bear a hundred years ago... when he was a baby."

"A hundred years ago? I heard that, young lady," Rafe muttered as he joined his young daughter on Jenny's front porch. "What are you doing over here, bothering Ms. Benjamin this early in the morning? I thought I told you to stay home."

"I know, Daddy. But that was 'fore Grandpa found Bruiser in that box in the attic. Grandpa was looking for his naval."

"His what?" Rafe asked in confusion.

"His naval. You know, what he wore on that big ship he used to live on."

"His naval uniform," Rafe finally translated.

Cindy nodded. "Uh-huh. Only he couldn't find it. All he found was Bruiser. And he was gonna throw him away just cause his insides were falling out. I couldn't let him do that, Daddy. Bruiser asked me to help him. So I brought him to Jenny."

"Ms. Benjamin," Rafe corrected her.

"I told Cindy she could call me by my first name," Jenny inserted.

"Can my daddy call you Jenny, too?" Cindy asked.

"I suppose."

"And you can call him Rafe," Cindy declared. Leaning forward, she confidingly added, "That's his name, you know."

There was a moment of silence as Jenny looked at Rafe, who was wearing jeans and a thick sweatshirt. She noted the way his hair was damply slicked back, as if he'd just come from the shower. As a result, his angular cheekbones were even more noticeable, as was the shadow of stubble darkening his jaw.

As if reading her thoughts, Rafe rubbed his hand over his jawline. "Sorry about this. Cindy took off before I had a chance to shave this morning." Turning to his daughter, he said, "You, young lady, disobeyed orders."

"Only cause Bruiser needed 'mergency surgery," Cindy replied earnestly. "I didn't want him to die like Mommy died."

Jenny saw the lightning flash of pain in Rafe's eyes. That and the tightening of his jaw were the only signs he gave of what Jenny knew had to be his inner turmoil as a result of his daughter's words.

"Did I do right, Daddy?" Cindy's voice was uncertain now. "You're not mad, are you?"

Rafe hunkered down to hug her. "No, I'm not mad that you tried to help Bruiser, but you shouldn't disobey me when I tell you to stay home. And you shouldn't be bothering Jenny this early in the morning."

"She wasn't bothering me," Jenny assured him. "Miriam and I were just getting ready to go to work but we hadn't actually started yet."

"Where do you work?" Cindy asked with the natural curiosity of a five-year-old.

"For the time being, I'm going to be working in my dining room. But once the barn is done, we'll be working out there."

"Making teddy bears, right?" Cindy said.

"That's right," Jenny confirmed.

Cindy turned to Rafe and said, "She makes teddy bears, Daddy."

"So she told me last night," Rafe replied.

"You and my daddy were dating last night?" Cindy asked with equal measure of surprise and delight, looking first at her father and then at Jenny.

"No, we weren't on a date," Jenny hurriedly assured her, noting the curious look Miriam was giving her. Knowing the other woman as well as she did, Jenny expected that Miriam would demand a complete explanation later.

"Why not?" Cindy asked.

"Because..." Jenny trailed off, uncertain of what to say.

"Yes?" Rafe prompted, clearly enjoying the dilemma in which Jenny found herself.

She shot him an irritated look. "*You* tell her."

"We haven't gone on a date yet, but we will soon," Rafe had the nerve to say to Cindy.

"Good." Cindy grinned her approval. "Cause I like Jenny. You like her too, right, Daddy?"

"Right, pumpkin."

"So when you are gonna go dating?" Cindy demanded.

Rafe turned his daughter's question right over to Jenny. "So when are we gonna go dating?" he repeated to Jenny with a wicked grin.

"Maybe in the year 2000," she muttered.

"That's too long. I'll be old by then," Cindy replied. "And you and my daddy'll be *ancient* by then!"

"Thanks a lot, kiddo," Rafe retorted.

It was his rueful look, the one he shared with Jenny, that got to her where nothing else could have. It was very hard for her to resist a man who laughed at himself.

As if sensing her moment of weakening, Rafe said, "How about joining Cindy and me for a picnic on Monday? The restaurant is closed and Cindy's got a day off school for teacher's conferences. We could make an afternoon of it— go take a drive up to Mount Washington or something. What do you say?"

Jenny should have said no. Politely, but firmly. And she fully intended to until she saw the eager look of anticipation in Cindy's eyes. Monday was normally a workday for her, but things wouldn't really be up and running for another two weeks or so. During this interim time she supposed she could take an afternoon off, especially in light of the fact that she was working most weekends on her designs and on creating her line of Bambino bears. But there was still so much to do before the barn was completed....

The five-year-old Cindy began getting impatient with Jenny's woolgathering and tugged on Jenny's hand to get her attention. "Don' you like my daddy?" the little girl demanded.

What could Jenny say but "Of course I do...."

"Good," Rafe inserted. "Then we'll pick you up at eleven-thirty on Monday morning. We'll bring the food. See you then. Come on, kiddo. Time for us to get back home."

Cindy only had time to thrust the bedraggled Bruiser into Jenny's arms before she and Rafe were gone, leaving Jenny wondering how she'd ended up agreeing to go on a picnic with them. Actually she *hadn't* agreed per se, but that hadn't stopped Rafe from barreling right on and getting what he wanted.

"So, who was that masked man that rode in here?" Miriam demanded with a big grin.

"My neighbor." Jenny closed the door before carefully placing Bruiser on the heavy Victorian curved sideboard that had come with the house since it was too heavy for anyone to pick up and move.

"They don't have neighbors like that in my neck of the woods," Miriam noted in between sighs.

"Don't let Max hear you talking like that," Jenny said, referring to Miriam's husband of the past thirty years.

"I'm happily married, not dead," Miriam replied. "And you'd have to be dead not to notice that man's—"

"Miriam..." Jenny said warningly, knowing the older woman's predilection for plain talking as well as her wicked sense of humor.

"Eyes. I was going to say eyes."

"Sure you were."

"Although I will confess that he fills out a pair of jeans quite nicely. I liked the shadowy jaw, too. Unshaven he had that untamed look, you know what I mean?"

Jenny could have told Miriam that Rafe had that untamed look even when he was clean shaven, but instead she said, "Don't go getting any ideas. He's just Cindy's father."

"How long ago did he lose his wife?"

"She died when Cindy was just a baby."

"Poor man." The other woman's look of compassion was soon replaced with one of speculation. "So your next-door neighbor is a handsome widower with a small daughter. Definite possibilities there." Miriam nodded approvingly.

"Trust me, he's only interested in my property."

Miriam blinked in surprise. "Excuse me?"

"You heard me. He came over last night offering to buy me out so he could expand his restaurant on my land."

"What did you tell him?"

"That I wasn't interested."

"Well, he seemed interested. In *you.*"

"I wouldn't put it past him to think he could charm me into selling my property to him," Jenny muttered.

"If you think that then why did you agree to go out with him?"

Jenny shifted uncomfortably. "I didn't agree, exactly."

"You didn't exactly refuse, either," Miriam pointed out.

"I didn't want to hurt Cindy's feelings."

"That was noble of you."

"I was just being nice," Jenny maintained.

"Of course you were," Miriam agreed with a mocking grin. "You're a very nice person. Extremely nice, even. *And* noble."

"Noble-schmoble," Jenny retorted, using one of Miriam's favorite turns of expression. "Let's get back to work."

Monday came all too soon, as far as Jenny was concerned. She'd been tempted a thousand times over the busy weekend to call Rafe's restaurant and leave a message canceling their supposed date. But the memory of that look in Cindy's eyes prevented her. She didn't have the heart to disappoint the little girl.

It was just one afternoon, she told herself. What could it hurt? Besides, she could use the break. She'd worked most of the weekend, sketching out some new designs, creating a new Bambino Bear, as well as beginning the repairs on Bruiser, Rafe's teddy bear.

While working on one of Bruiser's loose ears that morning, sewing it back in place with tiny stitches, she tried to picture what kind of little boy Rafe had been. Full of the devil, no doubt. Had he been born with that devil-may-care confidence or was that something he'd developed along the way? Had he grown up with any brothers or sisters? Or was he an only child, like herself?

It wasn't wise for her to get too curious about her handsome neighbor, Jenny reminded herself. She'd been half hoping that it would rain today, which would have taken care of their picnic date right there. But no, the day had dawned clear and sunny and promised to stay that way.

If she was going to go on this picnic thing, she needed to decide what to wear, and quickly, Jenny noted as she set the partially repaired Bruiser on the table. Rafe and Cindy would be there in less than an hour. She'd have to finish her work on Bruiser tomorrow.

Jenny settled on a pair of black slacks and a chenille turtleneck sweater in blue interspersed with flecks of colors ranging from red to green. The sweater's long tunic length and loose fit made it one of Jenny's favorites. A pair of black suede hiking boots completed her outfit.

After several attempts at doing something with her hair—from gathering it up into a ponytail to pinning it back with a barrette—she ended up grabbing a black suede headband and sliding that onto her head. At least it kept her shoulder-length hair from falling into her face too much.

Jenny was ready on time. Eleven-thirty came and went with no sign of Rafe and Cindy.

Jenny told herself she was relieved. Maybe it meant the picnic had been called off. Even so, she kept looking at the clock every two minutes. At eleven-forty-five, her doorbell rang.

"Sorry we're late," Rafe apologized.

"It was 'cause of Boots," Cindy declared.

"Boots?" Jenny repeated, looking down at the miniature athletic shoes the girl was wearing along with her jeans and sweatshirt.

"Boots is her cat," Rafe explained. "She went missing this morning."

"But we found her," Cindy inserted. "She's real good at hide-'n-go seek."

"She's good at the hiding part anyway," Rafe noted dryly.

"I was afraid she ran away, but she's sleeping behind the drapes."

"Near the hot-air duct," Rafe added. "That cat knows when it's got it good."

"Boots is a girl cat, Daddy. Not an *it*. You shouldn't call her *it*. She can't have kittens no more," Cindy added woefully for Jenny's benefit. "But she's still a girl cat."

"I'm sure she is," Jenny replied.

"You can come over and meet her, if you want," Cindy said. "Boots can't go outside. She likes it inside best."

"Like I said, the cat knows when she's got it good," Rafe said. "So are you ready to go?" Rafe asked Jenny.

She nodded.

It came as no surprise to her that Rafe was driving a four-wheel-drive Jeep, a vehicle that had the same kind of down-to-earth ruggedness that Rafe possessed.

What did surprise her was the hidden heat his touch provoked within her as he helped her step up into the Jeep's passenger side. He had one hand on her arm and his other on her back, and Jenny felt the imprint of each finger as if they'd been branded into her. She actually got goose bumps, which she immediately blamed on the weather—a lame excuse since it was a balmy sixty-five out.

Once settled in her seat, she avoided his gaze, fearing he might see how flustered she was. Instead she focused her attention on the interior of his Jeep. She'd heard that you could tell a lot about a man by the way he kept his car. There were no fuzzy dice hanging from the rearview mirror, no garter belt, either. But then Rafe was a widower with a small daughter, a father, a settled member of the business community—who happened to move with the stealth and grace of a cat burglar. He'd done so now, joining her in the Jeep without her even being aware of it.

Seeing him raising his eyebrows at her apparent interest in her surroundings, Jenny felt compelled to say something. "It's a nice Jeep" was all she could come up with.

"I just washed and cleaned it earlier this morning in your honor," he told her.

"You didn't have to do that."

"Yes, I did. I had junk piled all over the back seat, including new menus I just got printed up. Comes with the territory of running a restaurant. You okay back there, pumpkin?" Rafe asked, looking in the rearview mirror to see if Cindy had her seat belt on yet.

"Fine, daddy. How's Bruiser doing?" Cindy asked Jenny. "Did you make him all better yet?"

"Just about. He should be ready for you to take home by tomorrow. You're lucky Cindy saved your bear for you," Jenny told Rafe.

"Why's that?"

"Because it's a Steiff bear."

"Come again?"

"The bear is a Steiff bear. That's what the tag in its ear meant."

"Is that what that meant? When I was a kid my dad told me it was Bruiser's dog tags. I think he picked it up for me while he was in port in Germany."

"That would make sense. Steiff bears are made in Germany. Once he's back in shape, you really should hang on to him."

"You're telling me that teddy bears are actually worth something?"

"They're worth a great deal. Not only in monetary value, although that is some people's main consideration these days," Jenny muttered darkly. "You know it was Oscar Wilde who once said that 'Nowadays people know the price of everything and the value of nothing.'"

"Exactly what kind of monetary value are we talking about here?" Rafe wanted to know.

"Some of the earliest Steiff bears have gone for up to almost seven thousand dollars at auction."

Rafe whistled.

"Those are in mint condition, of course, and much older than yours," she added.

"According to Cindy, it's hard to get much older than me or Bruiser." Rafe winced, realizing he probably should have said "Bruiser and I" to be grammatically correct. And something about Jenny made him think of correctness. He was willing to bet she always got her tenses right and never screwed up. A college graduate, no doubt. One who quoted Oscar Wilde at him. Some fancy Ivy League school had probably given her that polish.

As for him, he liked to say that he'd attended the School of Hard Knocks. Sure he'd taken some courses in accounting and business techniques at night in the local community college but he'd never gotten a four-year degree. Hell, there hadn't been the time or the money. He supposed he could have looked into scholarships more, but the truth was that he got restless in a classroom.

He'd learned more by bumming around the world for a year or two than he ever could out of a textbook. And he'd certainly done his share of traveling, starting at an early age—ten different states in as many years during his childhood. His dad had eventually gotten stationed at Great Lakes naval base near Chicago, and that's where Rafe spent his teenage years.

It seemed like a lifetime ago now, he noted, looking at Cindy as he turned around to back the Jeep out of the driveway. He'd worked his way from the bottom up in the restaurant business—from busboy while he'd still been in high school, to working as a waiter on a cruise ship out of Florida, to manager of a place in New York City, to finally owning his own place. That had been a goal for longer than he could remember. To have his own place and be his own boss.

His rosy picture of the future had also included having Susan at his side, but his wife had died before their daughter's first birthday. So much for game plans.

Not that Susan's mother, Althea, had even credited him enough to have had a game plan. The truth was that his mother-in-law had never thought him good enough for her "golden girl," and to this day actually blamed him for Susan's death, as if he'd been responsible for the cancer that had eaten away at his wife's strength. Althea didn't approve of one single thing about him—never had, never would—including the way he was raising Cindy.

"Daddy, how long 'til we get there?" Cindy piped up to ask.

"We haven't even left the driveway yet, kiddo."

"I know. But how long 'til we get there?"

"You know, it occurs to me that I don't even know where we're going on this picnic of ours," Jenny pointed out.

"I thought we'd take a drive up Mount Washington first to build our appetite," Rafe replied.

"I like it there. It's on top of the world," Cindy informed Jenny.

Although Jenny knew of the mountain, she wasn't sure of its exact location. "Is it a long drive from here?"

Rafe shook his head. "Just down the road a bit. I keep forgetting you're not a native of these parts."

"It shows, does it?"

"You don't have the right accent," he told her.

"I'm from Connecticut originally."

"Ah."

"What's the 'ah' for?"

"A lot of wealthy families in Connecticut."

"That's true," she agreed. "But ours wasn't one of them."

"It wasn't?"

"Certainly not. My dad took off when I was six, so my mom had to move back home with her parents and go out to work in order to support us. She died when I was nine and my grandparents raised me." Jenny fell silent as she realized how much of her life she'd just let slip. Not that it was any big secret, but she generally didn't go around telling strangers about her father's desertion. And Rafe was still a stranger to her, neighbor or not. Feeling uncomfortable, she quickly changed the subject. "So tell me more about Mount Washington."

"It's not for the faint of heart," Rafe replied.

"Meaning what? We're going to be *climbing* the mountain?"

"We'll be climbing it in the Jeep."

"There is a road, I presume?"

"Sure there's a road."

"Good." She'd had visions of them bumping across some kind of wilderness trail.

"'Course, after you've traveled on the road, they give you a bumper sticker that says I Survived The Mount Washington Road," Rafe added. "Not afraid of heights, are you?"

"I don't know," she had to admit.

He smiled a knowing kind of smile. "Guess we'll find out," he murmured.

Jenny had a feeling that was just one of many things she was about to find out that afternoon.

Chapter Three

"**P.T.** Barnum called this—" Rafe indicated the view from the summit of Mt. Washington with a sweep of his hand "—the second greatest show on earth."

Jenny tried, with no success, to concentrate on the view and not the slender strength of Rafe's fingers. A man's hands were a personal weakness of hers, particularly hands that were lean and artistic the way Rafe's were.

During the ride up on the mostly gravel road built in the 1860s, Jenny discovered that she wasn't faint of heart nor was she afraid of heights—a good thing since the road had few barriers along the sheer edges and was steep enough to put the fear of God in most folks. One thing did make her more than a tad apprehensive, however, and that was this sensually charged tension she felt whenever she was near Rafe. She wasn't normally the type to be easily rattled by a man...or a simple thing such as his hands.

However, she was an artist, Jenny reminded herself, which meant that it was natural and perfectly acceptable for her to objectively appreciate the beauty of the masculine form. The problem was that she was appreciating Rafe's masculine form a little *too* much for comfort as he leaned into the back of the Jeep. Nice *tush,* as Miriam would say. Jenny grinned.

"Here—" Rafe straightened from his bent-over position, holding a sweatshirt in his hand "—put this on. It's cold up here." He tugged the huge cardigan-type sweatshirt around her, zipping it up for her the second she'd slipped her arms into the armholes. "At six thousand feet it stays cold even in the summer—never gets much above freezing."

"The wind doesn't help any," Jenny noted with a shiver.

Rafe tugged the sweatshirt's hood up over her head, tying it under her chin as if she were no older than his daughter. But the look he gave her was definitely mature, stormy and hungry.

She reached up to push a stand of hair out of her eyes, only to find that the sweatshirt sleeves were so long that her hands disappeared beneath the cuffs. With surprising gentleness, Rafe smoothed her hair away for her, his fingertips brushing against the chilled skin of her cheek and leaving a trail of fire.

Jenny held her breath, momentarily mesmerized. Then the sound of Cindy's childish laughter jerked her back to reality.

Realizing she hadn't yet registered the view, Jenny made a point of doing so now, studying it intensely, as if there would be a test later. They were well above the tree line here so there was nothing to soften the hard desolation of the bare rocks. In contrast, the surrounding mountains were soft waves of smoky blue, stretching far into the distance like bony contours of the earth's rounded spine.

"Being up here always puts things into perspective for me, you know?" Rafe murmured softly. "Makes me realize there's a big world out there even though it doesn't always feel like it."

Jenny's attention was drawn from the impressive scenery to the equally rugged planes of his face. His expression was a tad sad, a tad brooding—and totally fascinating. She wondered what had brought that look to his face. There were hidden depths to this man, but a woman would be foolish to think she'd be able to reach them without a pick and shovel. He was ... intense; she didn't know how else to put it. Like a mountain with a core of molten lava at its center.

She was doing it again—daydreaming. Time to focus on something practical, she silently chastised herself before finding a sign posted nearby that did the trick nicely. "I was right about it being windy up here. The highest wind ever observed was recorded here at two hundred and thirty-one miles per hour, a world record," Jenny said.

"How can you observe the wind?" Rafe countered with a slow smile.

"Things can be felt even if they can't be seen." Like the force field she stumbled into each time she got close to him, Jenny mentally added. Invisible but potent. "In fact, sometimes they're the strongest force of all."

"Can we go on the train, Daddy?"

Once again Cindy interrupted them, for which Jenny was eternally grateful. She needed some time to recover from the magnetic power of Rafe's gaze.

"No, the train isn't working right now," Rafe told his daughter.

"I had no idea a cog railway went up here," Jenny noted.

Rafe nodded. "It's the world's first cog railway."

"And it's still running? I'm impressed. They certainly don't build them like that anymore."

"Things rarely last these days," Rafe confirmed, the darkness in his eyes reminding her of a cloud passing over the sun. She wondered if he was thinking of his wife and how their happiness hadn't lasted. And then she found herself wondering what it would be like to have someone love you that way.

Uncomfortable with her thoughts, Jenny hurried over to the long wooden staircase leading back down to the parking lot. She wasn't sure of the cause; perhaps it was the altitude, perhaps it was the fact that she'd skipped breakfast— but she suddenly felt very, very dizzy.

Catching hold of her arm, Rafe said, "Whoa, there! Be careful." She momentarily leaned against him, grateful for his support. "Wouldn't want you falling down. First your rickety back steps and now here." He shook his head at her. "You're a hazard around stairs, you know that?"

And such was her lot in life, Jenny noted dryly. Other women were sirens. She was a hazard. She wasn't the kind of woman men got excited about. Never had been, never would be. She was more the girl-next-door type, or so she'd been told more times than she cared to remember by everyone—from her dentist to her last boyfriend.

No, she wasn't the type to grab a man's attention. So there had to be something else at work here, some other reason for Rafe's attempt to charm her. It had to be her land he was interested in. All this attention Rafe was giving her was his way of romancing her into agreeing to sell him her property. She'd be wise not to fall for his act, literally or figuratively.

Regaining her balance, she eased herself away from him. "I skipped breakfast and got dizzy for a minute. Were we going to eat up here?" she inquired prosaically.

"No, I had somewhere cozier in mind," Rafe told her.

Jenny wasn't sure she liked the sound of that, but she reminded herself that there wasn't much Rafe could do with his five-year-old daughter as a chaperon—for which she was *very* grateful.

The cozier place Rafe had in mind turned out to be in a stand of trees off the main highway leading back to town. Yellow- and red-tinted leaves provided a colorful blanket upon which Rafe spread an old quilt. Autumn was Jenny's favorite time of year. She considered the chromatic displays put on by Mother Nature to signal a new beginning rather than an end.

As Rafe and Cindy sat close together, their heads together as they looked into the large wicker basket, Jenny was struck by the picture they made. And she felt that hollow ache in her heart she experienced whenever she saw a man being a father to a little girl. She'd taken enough psych courses and read enough self-help books to know that she was experiencing father loss—that this was something she'd missed while growing up.

Her grandfather had been a distant and somewhat gruff man, not into taking little girls onto his lap and cuddling them. He just hadn't been the loving type.

Rafe was clearly loving with Cindy. It was written all over his face when he looked at his daughter. The pride and the love shone in his eyes. The humor, too.

He enjoyed being a father. Jenny could see that.

"Oh, Daddy, look. Hugo packed the smelly cheese stuff!" Cindy wrinkled her small nose in distaste.

"Hugo is my chef," Rafe explained for Jenny's benefit. "He doesn't think any meal is complete unless it includes French cuisine. Even a picnic has to include Brie, crusty French bread and wine. A roast-beef sandwich and a beer would've been fine with me."

"Ever think of telling him that?" Jenny suggested.

"All the time," Rafe replied. "But then I bite my tongue. Hugo is rather high-strung, you see. And he's the best damn chef in the state."

"You said the d-word, Daddy," Cindy exclaimed. "You owe me a dime!"

"In an all-male household there has to be some kind of deterrent against swearing," Rafe ruefully informed Jenny even as he dug into his jeans pocket for a dime.

"I got fifty cents from Grandpa the other day," Cindy proudly announced, prying Jenny's attention away from the taut pull of the denim on Rafe's jeans, outlining his masculine form.

"He's doing better," Rafe said, finally handing over his dime to his daughter.

Cindy nodded her agreement. "He used to have to pay me two dollars in the beginning."

"He sounds like quite a character," Jenny noted, pleased that her voice wasn't as breathless as she felt. Whew! She was about ready to grab a paper napkin and fan herself here. Miriam was right, Rafe did fill out a pair of jeans *quite* nicely!

"Yeah, my pop's a character, all right," Rafe confirmed.

"Look, Daddy, Spud made us his potato salad. Goody! That's my favorite."

Jenny recalled Cindy telling her earlier that Spud was an old buddy of her grandfather's, a cook in the navy who'd joined the family when he'd retired.

"Spud and Hugo fight all the time," Cindy was saying. "Their faces go all red like the potato salad." The little girl pointed to the salad that was indeed tinted red from the beets included in the recipe. "Spud's got a tattoo but not as big as Grandpa's. It's just a snake one. I liked the naked lady one better. Grandpa can even move his arm and make the naked lady dance. You should see it!"

"It sounds impressive," Jenny said.

"What's that mean?" Cindy asked.

"Nice, only better," Jenny replied.

"I think *you're* impressive," Cindy said, careful to get the word right. "Don't you think so, too, Daddy?"

"Sure do."

Jenny knew one thing that was impressive and that was Rafe's effect on her. He was sitting a good two feet away, yet he was still able to make her feel warm and tingly all over.

He didn't even attempt to cloak his stare in courtesy. It was blatant and approving without being insulting—no easy feat. Jenny had never been looked at in such a way.

"You're not eating, Daddy. Aren't you hungry?"

"I'm starving," Rafe replied, his eyes on Jenny, his voice seductively soft and rough.

"*I'm* not on the menu." Jenny's murmured warning was for his ears only.

"I never said you were," he returned.

"No, but you were looking at me the way a hungry man would eye his last meal."

"You've got a vivid imagination. Must come in handy in your line of work."

"I may have a vivid imagination, but I've also got both feet firmly planted on the ground. I've got a practical streak a mile wide," she informed him.

"A mile wide, huh?"

"That's right," she confirmed. "I'm not the type to be swept off my feet."

"Maybe you just haven't had the right man do the sweeping," Rafe countered. "You want spicy or mild?"

Jenny blinked at him. What kind of question was that? "Excuse me?"

"Roast beef." He held up two plastic containers. "I've got spicy or mild. Which do you prefer?"

"Oh. Mild, I guess."

"I figured as much. For bread we've got kaiser rolls, rye bread and, of course, Hugo's French bread."

"French bread is good."

"Ah, a bit of daring. Bravo. Do you want mustard or mayonnaise on that?"

"Both."

He raised an eyebrow at her. "And tomato?"

"Yes, thank you. Lettuce, too," she added, forestalling his next question.

She held her hand out, palm up, for the plate and sandwich he was about to give her.

"What did you do to your finger?" Rafe asked, frowning at the angry red wound on her fingertip.

"Occupational hazard," Jenny noted ruefully. "That and a sore back. I pricked myself with a needle."

Before she could guess his intentions, Rafe lifted her fingers to his lips and kissed her injury. The feel of his lips on her skin made her sensitized nerve endings vibrate.

"Just like Sleeping Beauty," Cindy declared with a big grin on her face. "Her finger bleeded, too, and the prince kissed her."

For a few brief moments there, Jenny had actually forgotten the little girl's presence, so potent had the interaction been between Rafe and herself. Snatching her hand away, Jenny noted as she did so that her fingertip still hummed where he'd kissed it.

She had to remind herself that she knew what he was up to, what he was after. And it wasn't her. It was her property. As long as she kept that firmly in mind, she could afford to sit back and enjoy watching him work at trying to charm her.

Yet for some reason she got the impression Rafe wasn't a man who made a habit of getting by on his charm. He was too direct for that, too impatient. But he was also a man to whom the ends justified the means. A man who knew what he wanted and went after it.

So when he drove her home later that afternoon and mistakenly drove into his own driveway instead of hers, it came as no surprise to Jenny that he invited her inside.

"No thanks," she replied. "I've got some work to catch up on."

"If you're sure..."

"I'm sure."

"Then I'll walk you home. You go on inside, Cindy," Rafe told his daughter. "Go show Grandpa the pretty leaves you found."

Smooth move, Jenny thought to herself. Rafe clearly didn't want his daughter around to act as chaperon any longer.

"You're smiling," Rafe noted, reaching out to ever so lightly brush his fingertips across her lips.

The resulting sizzle along her nerve endings was enough to make her nervous. "Am I?"

Rafe nodded. "You *were*. Now you look like a scared rabbit."

"Gee, thanks." Jenny frowned and gave him a dark look of displeasure. "Anyone ever tell you you've got a real way with words?"

"No, but a woman with fire in her eyes and a huge bear in her hands did accuse me of being antisocial once."

"You do have a way of trying to steamroll people to make them do what you want. Like my going out on this picnic with you today," she reminded him as they climbed the steps to her front door.

"Come on, the day wasn't so bad, was it?" Rafe countered.

"Not so bad, no."

"Neither is this...." Cupping her chin in his hand, Rafe swooped down to kiss her.

Jenny thought she'd been ready for him. She'd suspected he'd gotten rid of Cindy for precisely this reason—so that he could kiss her without an audience. She'd been prepared...until his lips brushed hers, softly, seductively, slowly.

That's when Jenny realized in dazed dismay that she'd never really been kissed before; it was as simple as that. For if a kiss meant that your very soul sang, then she'd been completely in the dark...until now. For now sweet music throbbed in every fiber of her being.

This was big—monumental! This was what made mere men poets and launched a thousand ships. This was... incredibly sexy and unbelievably tempting. It was just a kiss. But, oh, what a kiss...!

He pulled away just enough for her to see the slightly triumphant, albeit surprised, look in his eyes. It was enough to make her recover her shattered composure in record time. "You can kiss me all you want, but you won't change my mind about selling out to you," she told him.

"Kiss you all I want, hmm?" Rafe whispered, his breath warm on her moist lips. "I accept your challenge."

"It wasn't a—"

The rest of her words were lost under the expert tutelage of his mouth. As her lips softened and then parted, Rafe deepened their kiss, moving onto the next level of seduction. He was bolder this time, enticing her with the subtle motion of his tongue, yet careful not to overwhelm her. With each successive kiss he'd zero in on new territory—the corner of her mouth, the curve of her upper lip—all the while coaxing her into responding.

"Still not tempted?" he asked after their fifth kiss.

Jenny was tempted, all right! Tempted to kiss him again. But not tempted to sell. "That's right," she said bravely. "Still not tempted. Good night."

"I haven't given up," he warned her before she shut the door on him.

Given up on what? she wondered. Trying to tempt her into selling her property, or trying to just plain tempt her?

"So, how did your date go, son?" Rafe's dad, Chuck, asked him the moment he walked into their living quarters above the restaurant.

"Fine," Rafe said briefly.

"You've got lipstick on your face."

"I'm not seventeen anymore, Pop," he noted in irritation.

"I know you're not. You're a father yourself, with a daughter who asks more questions than Carter has little pills. She's been asking where babies come from again."

Rafe groaned. "What did you tell her?"

"I distracted her. Told her a joke. A good one, too. The one about the guy at the bar... Anyway, it worked. For now. But if she sees that lipstick and figures out that you've been kissing our lovely neighbor, she's bound to start asking questions again. Questions you may not want to answer."

Rafe knew all about questions he didn't want to answer. He had plenty of them himself. Such as why he'd kissed Jenny the way he had. Why she intrigued him the way she did. Why he couldn't seem to resist the challenge in her sky-blue eyes.

At first Rafe had justified his actions with the memory of how he'd been done out of the property old man Miller had promised to sell him, before the old geezer had pulled a fast one on him. Not that Rafe was egotistical enough to think he could just kiss Jenny and she'd agree to sell her land to him. He just thought that if he got to know her a little better he could come up with a way of getting his banquet hall built. After all, she could make teddy bears anywhere. He couldn't expand his restaurant anywhere else.

It appeared, however, that Jenny had seen right through him, which no doubt explained those amused smiles she'd given him throughout the day.

He should have called it a day and moved on. But he couldn't. The truth was that Jenny Benjamin had awakened a part of himself that he'd thought had died with Susan. She intrigued him. She'd caught his attention as nothing else had, aside from work and his family. It wasn't love, it couldn't be, but still he'd enjoyed the banter and their battle of wills.

"She's very strong-willed, even more stubborn than I thought," Rafe murmured to himself.

"Who is?" his father demanded.

"Our lovely neighbor."

"You mean you're having trouble handling her? That would be a first, you not getting something you set out after. Not that anyone has ever handed you anything on a silver platter, mind you. I raised you to work for what you wanted. And you always have. Worked for it and gotten what you wanted."

"Not always," Rafe noted with quiet bitterness. "I didn't want Susan to die."

"I know. And you worked hard to make sure Susan got the best care possible, despite what that crazy mother of hers says. The woman called again while you were out."

"What did you tell her?"

"That you weren't home, that you were out with your daughter. She tried giving me an earful with one of those high-and-mighty lectures of hers, as if she's an expert on child rearing." Chuck snorted. "Only reason Susan turned out as sweet as she did is 'cause she was raised by a nanny, and not that witch of a woman."

"I agree."

"But sweet as she was, Susan's not with us any longer. She's been gone over four years now. It's time you got on with your life, son. That's why I was so pleased you're finally dating again. You haven't gone out much since... Anyway, maybe you found someone new...." Chuck's voice trailed off at the fiery look Rafe gave him.

"It almost destroyed me when Susan died," Rafe grated. "I'm not gonna go through something like that again, Pop."

"The chances of another woman you love dying..."

"You don't understand. There won't ever be another woman I'll love. There can't be. End of discussion."

"Where the heck did those sketches go?" Jenny muttered as she searched the drawing table for the third time. Unable to settle down after the kisses she'd shared with

Rafe, she'd finally decided she might as well try and direct all this nervous energy toward getting some work done.

It was only when she sat down at her angled drawing table that Jenny realized that her designs appeared to have been rearranged and some were missing altogether. "They can't have gotten up and walked off on their own," she grumbled.

Her search was interrupted by a phone call. Her voice reflected her impatience as she answered it.

"Leave," a muffled male voice said.

"Get a life," she shot right back before hanging up the phone with a decisive bang. "Stupid teenagers," she muttered, before returning to her hunt for her missing sketches. "I can't believe I lost those papers. They must be here somewhere."

But they weren't. She searched the dining room area where her desk was temporarily located, before widening her inspection to include the entire lower floor. Since she still hadn't unpacked all her belongings and had little furniture, the search didn't take long. She even went upstairs and checked beside her bed on the off chance she might have carried the sketches upstairs to look at last night before she'd gone to sleep. Nothing. No sign of the newest Bambino Bear sketches she'd been working on.

Most of the time Jenny worked with the material and the bears themselves as she tried out new designs, working on them as if they were soft sculptures she was molding. But sometimes she used sketches for design ideas.

It was a good thing this particular design hadn't been one she'd meant to go with, but still it was disconcerting to have something disappear like that. Almost as disconcerting as it had been to have had Rafe kissing her. The man had incredible lips. She'd had no idea a kiss could rock her so deeply, shaking her to her soul.

Maybe it was hormones. Or a full moon. She tried to come up with something, anything that would explain her reaction. It wasn't as if Rafe had been the first man to ever kiss her—he was just the first man to ever kiss her senseless. The other kisses she'd experienced paled in comparison. Paled...? Heck, they completely evaporated! By contrast, the feel of Rafe's mouth moving over hers was permanently etched in her memory bank.

"I haven't given up," Rafe had warned her, and he was true to his word. He dropped by or called several times over the next few days.

Jenny kept meaning to return the newly repaired Bruiser to him, but kept forgetting. A Freudian slip, she told herself as she restlessly turned in her bed at night. Hanging on to Rafe's teddy bear meant she was hanging on to him. Every night she vowed to free herself from his spell by giving him his darn bear back, and every morning she forgot to do it. She excused herself by saying she had a lot on her mind these days. It was certainly true.

As if the issues of Rafe and his effect on her weren't complicating enough, Jenny was also running into problems with her business. It seemed as if everything that could go wrong had. Two more delivery shipments had gotten screwed up and now it looked to her as if it would take a miracle to get the renovation work on the barn completed on time.

"You're sure you're going to have everything done by the deadline?" Jenny asked the contractor for the fifth time in as many days.

"Yep," Mr. Gardner laconically replied.

"That's what you said five days ago, and you're not much further along now than you were then."

The older man just shrugged. "Can't control the weather."

"It's been sunny for the past five days, Mr. Gardner."

"Rain was in the forecast. Twenty-percent chance."

"Look, Mr. Gardner, let me put it this way. You either have this project finished when we agreed or I won't be paying you."

He frowned at her. "Now don't go threatening me, girlie. I was building buildings before you were born."

"And you're probably still building them without finishing a single one!" she shot back.

"If you don't like the way I'm doing the job, you're welcome to hire someone else."

Jenny had foreseen him threatening to pull out and leave her with the place in an uproar. It was the main reason she'd kept quiet as long as she had about his dallying construction ways. But she had an ace of her own up her sleeve. "If you're not capable of finishing the job, then I'll just hire Mr. Fadden to finish up."

A little investigating on her part had turned up the information that Mr. Gardner's brother-in-law had recently branched out on his own, creating quite a rivalry between the two men. Knowing human nature, particularly in the male of the species, she was willing to bet that Mr. Gardner wasn't about to let his brother-in-law have this job. She was right.

"Now there's no need for that," Mr. Gardner stated in a conciliatory tone of voice. "I can have a full crew here in fifteen minutes."

"Fine. You do that and you can keep the job. You don't and I'll have to call Mr. Fadden."

Mr. Gardner shoved back his cap with his thumb. "You know how to play hardball, don't you?"

"When I have to, yes."

"Don't you worry. We'll get this job done or my name isn't Herbert Gardner."

Jenny narrowed her eyes suspiciously. "I thought your first name was Henry?"

"Er, I mean Henry."

"No more dragging your feet on this project, Mr. Gardner. I won't warn you again. I'll just hire your brother-in-law. Are we clear on that?"

"Clear as ice."

"Good. I'm glad we've got that settled."

Sure enough, fifteen minutes later the barn was crawling with workmen, busily nailing and hammering and sawing. Jenny left the pandemonium behind, as she returned to the house where Miriam was waiting, applauding her.

"What was that for?" Jenny asked.

"For laying down the law to that shyster contractor Gardner. I wouldn't trust that *momzer* any further than I could toss him."

"You're gonna have to translate that last one for me, Miriam," Jenny noted. Most of Miriam's Yiddish expressions Jenny had picked up and understood in time, but this was a new one for her.

"Let's just say he's no *mensch*."

Jenny knew a *mensch* was someone who was honorable and trustworthy.

"Unlike your neighbor," Miriam continued. "You know, the good-looking one. Now *he's* a *mensch*. And he's been dropping by a lot lately, hasn't he?"

"I told you—"

"I know. He's interested in your...property."

"Why do I get the impression you're not talking about the same kind of property I am?"

"Because I've seen the way the man looks at you."

"Like he'd like to shake some sense into me, you mean."

"That's just his Heathcliff look."

"His what?"

"His dark and brooding look. And I must say that on him it looks good."

"You're incorrigible."

"But I'm right."

"Okay, so on him, dark and brooding looks good. So what?"

"So why is he still coming over every day?"

"To drive me nuts."

"Exactly."

"So I'll sell out to him."

"That's one way of putting it."

"Miriam!"

"I couldn't help myself," the other woman said with an unrepentant grin.

"I don't want to talk about Rafe any longer," Jenny stated, rubbing her forehead where little men with jackhammers seemed to be at work. "It gives me a headache."

"That hammering and sawing out there would give anyone a headache."

"At least they're working again. For a while there, I wondered if they were going to finish in this millennium or the next one."

"But you set them straight. Good for you." Miriam patted her shoulder.

"I can be tough when I have to be," Jenny proclaimed. "I'm not going to let any stubborn, idiotic man hold me back!"

"This a private male-bashing party or can anyone join in?" Rafe dryly inquired from the threshold of the front foyer. "I knocked but you must not have heard me."

"Who could hear anything with that tumult out there?" Miriam countered. "I'm going to go get some aspirin. I'll be back shortly."

And so Jenny found herself alone with Rafe yet again.

"You don't have to look so apprehensive," Rafe stated. "I'm not going to ravish you. Not right here and now anyway."

"I wasn't looking apprehensive."

"Sure you were. Here." He took her by the shoulders and turned her so that she faced the foyer mirror. "Look at this face."

"I'd rather not," she retorted.

Standing close behind her, Rafe met her eyes in the mirror. "Why not? It's a nice face."

Nice, she thought to herself. Right. Just what every woman wants to hear. She wrinkled her nose.

"You have a little bit of a nose, do you know that?" he murmured.

"Careful, or your lavish compliments will go to my head," she noted mockingly.

"And your mouth." Rafe brushed his thumb over her full bottom lip, never taking his eyes from hers where they remained linked in the fathomless mystery of the mirror. "When you're about to dig in your heels, you do that thing with your lower lip... Ah, you're doing it now. See?"

What Jenny *saw* was Rafe in the mirror, looking lean and slightly dangerous in a black sweater and black jeans. She willed her heartbeat to remain normal, to no avail. Her breathing was fast, as well, which meant that each time she inhaled, her back brushed against his chest and primitive heat encompassed her. "I know exactly what you're doing, you know," Jenny informed him.

He raised one eyebrow, which gave him an even more satirical look. "You do?"

"Of course."

"And what it is you think I'm trying to do?"

"Charm me."

"And am I succeeding?"

"Absolutely not."

"Why not?"

"Why not?" she repeated, dumbfounded.

"If there's something wrong with my technique, I'd appreciate it if you'd tell me what it is."

"Your technique is fine and you darn well know it," she retorted, brushing his tempting hand away from its dangerous proximity to her lips.

"If my technique is so fine, then why isn't it working on you?"

It was working, to a certain extent, Jenny noted crossly. And she wasn't pleased about it. Not one bit. "I already told you that I'm not the kind of woman to be swept off my feet and charmed into doing something I don't want to do."

"How about charmed into doing something you *do* want to do?"

"I'm not going to sell my property to you, Rafe," she stated bluntly. "No matter how many times you try and sweet-talk me."

"I'm not getting anywhere, hmm?"

"That's right."

He brushed his index finger over the pulse fluttering along her throat. "And the reason your heartbeat is so fast . . . ?"

"Anger."

"Ah, anger. A strong emotion. Like desire. Or hunger."

"Or lust." Jenny could have bitten off her tongue for letting that slip.

"Really? Tell me more. I had no idea you felt that way."

"I don't!"

"No?"

"Absolutely not!"

"Am I interrupting something?" Miriam asked hopefully.

"No, of course not," Jenny hurriedly assured her as she stepped away from Rafe.

"I was just trying to show Jenny her true self," Rafe replied.

"Did it work?" Miriam asked.

"Only time will tell," Rafe said before sauntering out.

* * *

Sunday was supposed to be a day of rest. A day of relaxation. But it was hard for Jenny to either rest or relax when there was so much to worry about: Rafe, her reaction to him, the series of mishaps with her company. She preferred concentrating on the work problems and avoiding the subject of Rafe, but she couldn't ignore the possibility that the two might be connected.

Because there was no way that so *many* things could go wrong on their own—missing shipments, lost designs, building delays—it all added up to suspicions of sabotage. With those thoughts in mind, she left her house down the rickety back steps Mr. Gardner had yet to repair although he said he'd get to it soon.

"I thought I told you to get those stairs fixed," Rafe commented.

Jenny almost jumped out of her skin. "I wish you'd stop doing that!" she exclaimed, her hand going to her heart—which was racing.

"Doing what?"

"Sneaking up on me like that. What are you doing awake this early in the morning, anyway? I thought you'd be sleeping in after the busy night you had at Murphy's last night."

"Sleeping in? You obviously haven't lived with a five-year-old. They don't understand the concept."

"So what are you doing here?" Jenny asked him bluntly.

"My, someone's crabby this morning," he drawled.

"Yeah, well you'd be crabby, too, if you were having the problems I've been having," she retorted.

"What kind of problems?"

"Oh, your regular run-of-the-mill sabotage stuff." She turned to face him. "You wouldn't happen to know who might be trying to disrupt things around here, now would you? Someone who might be trying to scare me into selling out?" she mockingly inquired.

Rafe was displeased by her insinuation—she saw that immediately. Too bad. She was displeased, too—by this surge of awareness she felt whenever he was near.

"No, I wouldn't know," he retorted, his voice dark with anger. "I'm not into bullying and frightening defenseless women."

"No? What *do* you do to defenseless women?" she countered.

"When they're as stubborn and as impossible as you are, I do this—" Without further ado, Rafe pulled her in his arms and kissed her.

Chapter Four

Jenny was stunned. How had this happened? How had she ended up in his arms? Why hadn't she protested? Because it had happened too fast; his mouth had silenced hers before she could utter a word.

Her lips had been parted with a tiny gasp of surprise when he'd swooped down to kiss her. His mouth was now slanted across hers, the angle ensuring complete possession. Jenny tasted the swift force of his hunger... and found herself responding to it, blindly, unknowingly. When his tongue seductively slid past her lips, she met it with her own—tentatively at first and then with growing ardor.

She felt wild and free, as if she were standing on top of a mountain with the wind lashing its way through her. Rafe's hands were in her hair, his fingers spread out to cup the back of her head. The tempting motion of his fingers caressing her scalp was like that of a gentle tiger.

Her own hands had gone to his chest in a vain attempt to ward him off. Instead of pushing him away, she now shifted her hands along the warm cotton of his shirt. She was captured in the warm cocoon provided by his arms and his open jacket. When he tugged her closer, there was nowhere for her hands to go except around his waist, all the way to his back.

Even the wind couldn't have fit between them now. From shoulder to thigh, the heat of his body was indelibly imprinted onto hers. The ever-increasing force of their kiss soon impelled her head down onto his shoulder as the sultry imprisonment continued. With every thrust of his tongue he was driving her deeper into this whirlwind of raw passion.

She couldn't give in. She had to stop this. Gasping a protest as much of her own behavior as of his, she tore herself from his arms and whirled away from him. She was furious with herself for giving in and with him for tempting her to do so.

She stomped off toward the barn, stopping long enough to unlock the door while muttering dark threats to a certain man with dark looks. Shoving open the door, she stormed into the building only to stop short. The place was a mess!

Water was everywhere; all over the floor, dripping onto the worktables, soaking into the boxes she had stored against the wall. The wallboard on the north side, that had just been sealed the day before and looked so pristine, now had dark watermarks from ceiling to floor.

Stunned, Jenny stood there for a second, frozen in her tracks, looking at the flooded chaos in front of her without being able to fully comprehend it. Then she felt someone's presence behind her. Startled, she shrieked and twirled around to find Rafe standing there, the expression on his face one of fire and brimstone... and confusion. Then he went into action.

"Where's your water shut off?"

His curt question snapped her out of her temporary state of shock. "The water hasn't been turned on in here yet."

"What about electricity?"

"The electrician was going to come tomorrow to finish the wiring. Nothing has been hooked up yet. The workmen were using extension cords from my house, but they're not plugged in right now. I don't understand. Where could all this water have come from?"

Looking up, Rafe said, "The roof."

"The roof?" she repeated stupidly.

"Your roof leaked." He pointed to an area where they could see daylight. "After that heavy rain we had last night it poured straight in here."

"But Mr. Gardner never said anything about a problem with the roof."

Instead of replying to her comment, Rafe said, "Grab a corner of this table and we'll move it out of the way before it gets wet, too."

Jenny did as he ordered, her mind racing as she tried to assess the damage already done. She didn't know what to try and save first. The boxes of material on the bottom were goners.

"It's not as bad as it looks," she heard Rafe say.

"No, it's probably worse," she muttered, anger boiling deep within her. How could this have happened? She was supposed to be having the barn repaired, not destroyed. "This does it! I'm calling in reinforcements!"

"Where are you going?" Rafe called out as she stormed out of the barn.

"To do something I should have done several days ago— call Mr. Fadden and have him take over this job."

She was back five minutes later. "He said he'll be here shortly. And I also called Miriam. She and Max will be right over."

While she was gone, she saw that Rafe had moved some of the still-dry boxes in danger of getting wet either to higher locations or to the two safe corners of the barn.

"I've got a Wetvac you can borrow to get some of this water up from the floor," Rafe told her. "There's only a few inches of water, but it's spread over a large area. And I can give Spud a call to come help out."

"You don't have to do that...." Her voice trailed off as he tugged her around to face him.

"Surely you don't think I had anything to do with this, do you?" Rafe said.

The lost look in her eyes got to him, hitting him like a sucker punch in the gut. She was so pale. He already felt like a heel for kissing her the way he had, angrily grabbing her and yanking her into his arms like that. He certainly hadn't come over here this morning planning on kissing her. She'd *made* him do it, with that mocking insinuation of hers.

No, that wasn't right, Rafe wearily corrected himself. He was man enough to accept responsibility for his own actions. The truth was that he'd kissed her because she'd aggravated the hell out of him and because he was attracted to her. He wasn't sure what it was about her exactly—her husky fire-and-ice voice, her passionate approach to life, her luscious mouth—but he was intrigued. And she didn't trust him further than she could spit, which wasn't far since everyone knew that classy women like her couldn't spit worth squat.

He had to say something, anything to take that forlorn look out of her eyes. "Jenny..."

They were interrupted by the arrival of a new work crew. While Mr. Fadden directed his men onto ladders outside leading to the roof, Rafe went back to his place to get the Wetvac. By the time he returned, Miriam and her husband were there, helping Jenny sort through the wet boxes—trying to salvage what they could. "The curly mohair is a goner, but I think we can dry out the distressed mohair," Miriam was saying.

"It's even more distressed now," Jenny replied in a weak attempt at humor.

Rafe had to hand it to her, she'd bounced back well. Unfortunately, he didn't get a chance to speak to Jenny alone for the rest of the day as the barn was soon filled with several volunteers. Spud pitched in, but had to leave after two hours in order to take care of the lunch crowd at the restaurant. Rafe stayed where he was. Hugo and Spud could handle the lunch crowd on their own without World War III breaking out, or so he hoped. He was needed more here.

So what are you thinking, Rafe asked himself later that afternoon as he aimed a couple of electrical fans at the damp wallboard. That because you've helped out here, that will put you in Jenny's good graces? Knowing her, she'd probably think it was part of some master plan, a plan that called for him to deliberately get her into a jam simply so he could be there to rescue her. Then she'd be so grateful she'd do whatever he wanted. Yeah, right. That'd be the day. Not that he'd ever do such a thing in the first place.

Did she really think he was that devious? Rafe wondered with a frown. She never had answered his question, about whether or not she believed him responsible for this disaster.

She'd been working like a trooper all day, never sitting down once. He knew, because he'd tried to get her to rest and had almost gotten his head bitten off. He'd gotten the same reaction when he'd tried to get her to eat some of the lunch he'd had Spud drop by.

It was getting dark now and most of the volunteers had gone home. The worst of the damage had been cleaned up. Mr. Fadden and his crew had patched up the roof. The wooden flooring might not completely recover, but a majority of the planks hadn't warped. Jenny had had the presence of mind to take pictures before the cleanup operation had begun, so that she'd have something to show her insurance adjuster when he showed up in the morning.

After her initial shock of that morning, she'd been cool, calm and collected all day. Too collected, if you asked him, Rafe decided. The effort of all that restraint was starting to show. He could see it in the frozen fragility of her eyes, hear it in the polite brittleness of her voice. She had to be dog tired, but she showed no signs of letting up. Fatigue had washed all sign of color from her face, leaving her looking like a pale shadow of herself.

"Enough," Rafe growled, taking the mop from her hands. "There's nothing more you can do here tonight. We'll lock this place up and then you're going to come over to my place for some dinner. You haven't eaten a thing all day and you look ready to collapse."

"There you go again, trying to turn my head with fancy compliments," she mockingly retorted.

"Very funny. Come on." He tugged on her arm as if to lead her out himself.

Jenny stubbornly dug in her heels. "I'm not in the mood to dress up for dinner at your place. Frankly, I'm too tired."

"Who said anything about dressing up? This will be a private dinner." When she gave him a suspicious look, he added, "My father and Cindy will be there, as well." Seeing her hesitate, he threw in the clincher. "Hugo has prepared honey-baked ham with fresh asparagus and parsleyed new potatoes. And for dessert there's upside-down pineapple cake."

"I can't go over there looking like this." Her gesture indicated everything from her hair to her jeans, which were still rolled up around her slender ankles from her earlier excursions sloshing around the barn's flooded floor.

"You can clean up at the restaurant," Rafe said.

She shook her head. "I don't want everyone seeing me like this."

"Fine. We'll go in the back entrance and you can use the employees' washroom to clean up. Satisfied?" The look on his face warned her that even if she wasn't, she was coming with him because he wasn't taking no for an answer.

She didn't have the energy to keep arguing. Besides, the lack of food was catching up with her, making her light headed.

"You need a keeper," he muttered as she swayed. "Do you know that?" Placing an arm around her shoulders, he guided her out of the barn, taking the key from her and locking up for her.

He fussed at her all the way to his place, where he seemed prepared to take over her personal cleanup operations until she shooed him out of the washroom. Looking at her reflection in the small mirror, she had to admit that she'd looked better. As Jenny made good use of the soap and water, she reflected on the sweet pleasure of having a man like Rafe look after her. The previous men in her life hadn't been into protection, except of their own hides. Her grandfather hadn't had any patience with vulnerability of any kind. The bottom line was that she'd never had a man go out of his way to protect or take care of her.

She knew she shouldn't get used to it...and she wouldn't. But just for a moment or two, she allowed herself to bask in the soft warmth of being cared for.

After cleaning up, she felt a little better, although she wished Rafe hadn't hustled her over here so quickly—she would have liked to have stopped at home to at least pick up her purse. As it was, she had nothing: no makeup, no lipstick, not even a comb. Honesty compelled her to admit that had she stopped at home, she wouldn't have made it any farther. She was pretty beat.

When she opened the washroom door, she was greeted by the most delicious aromas—baked ham, pineapple and savory spices she couldn't put a name to but that made her mouth water and her stomach growl. The washroom was near the back door, so she hadn't actually seen the kitchen before. Now that she did, she was impressed by all the shining chrome and white surfaces, let alone the fancy equipment.

All in all, there was an air of organized chaos that Jenny recognized from her own waitressing days in college. The servers, dressed in white shirts and black pants, were efficiently taking trays full of dinners out through the swinging doors that must lead to the restaurant's main dining room.

"There you are," Rafe said. Taking her arm, he led her past the pots boiling on the huge commercial stove and stopped beside a man in a white chef's hat. He had a rubbery kind of face that was bent into a scowl at the moment. His hair, what she could see of it beneath the chef's hat, was dark and slicked back off his high forehead. "This is Hugo," Rafe said. "And this is Hugo's kitchen."

Jenny was uncertain of the proprieties here. Was she supposed to thank Hugo for allowing her in his kitchen? She made do by just saying, "Whatever you're cooking smells delicious, Hugo."

Apparently she'd said the right thing, because Hugo beamed and nodded as if she'd just passed a test. Then his expression darkened as he muttered, "I do the best I can in such cramped quarters."

"And you met Spud earlier," Rafe noted with a gesture in the older man's direction.

Spud grinned at her, his gold front tooth shining. He looked like a career navy cook, with a burly physique and a crew cut.

"Does everyone call you Spud or is there another name you'd prefer that I use?" Jenny asked him.

"Spud's the only name I answer to," he replied. "Got the nickname my first days in the navy, from all the KP duty I pulled peeling potatoes. And here I am—" he held up a potato in one hand and a peeler in another "—still peeling potatoes."

"And not doing a good job." Hugo sniffed. "You left skin on those." He pointed disdainfully to a potato on top of the colander.

"Don't sweat it, Hughie," Spud cheerfully replied. "The world's not a perfect place, ya know? Besides, a little peel in life is good for the soul."

"You have the soul of a peasant," Hugo declared dramatically.

"Better that than the soul of a wimp," Spud retorted.

Their imminent battle was interrupted by Cindy's arrival. "You're here! You're here!" Cindy looked so delighted that Jenny instinctively dropped to her knees as the little girl rushed over to hug her. "Come on...." Cindy tugged on Jenny's hand. "You gotta come see my room and all my toys."

"After dinner, kiddo," Rafe said. "Did you wash your hands before you came downstairs?"

"Yes, Daddy." She held them out for his inspection. "Did you ask her yet?"

"Ask me what?" Jenny said.

"Will you paint my nails for me?" Cindy blurted out in a rush. "No one here knows how. I got the polish and everything."

"Her grandmother got her one of those makeup kits for little girls," Rafe admitted. "She's been driving me nuts wanting to have her nails polished."

"Daddy says boys don't know how to do those things."

"They can learn," Jenny replied, with a look in Rafe's direction.

"I don't want my daddy learning on me, though," Cindy stated.

Good point. Jenny couldn't fault her there.

"So will you do it for me?" Cindy repeated.

"Sure," Jenny agreed.

"After dinner," Rafe added, seeing the light in his daughter's eyes.

"I could eat better if my nails was polished, Daddy," she stated with a winsome look.

Rafe shook his head in amazement. He had no idea where his daughter had picked up that little feminine ploy of batting her eyelashes and looking at him that way. She certainly hadn't picked it up from the masculine company she spent much of her time in. She'd had this trick in her arsenal before she'd started kindergarten last month, so he couldn't attribute it to that, either.

"Nice try, but no cigar," Rafe told his daughter, tweaking her nose as he did so.

"So you're our mysterious new neighbor?" a gravelly voice boomed out as a man with a headful of white hair and a devilish gleam in his blue eyes joined them. "I'm Chuck, Rafe's father. Glad to meet you after all this time." Chuck pumped her hand up and down, as if she were an old-fashioned water pump. "I've been hearing a lot about you."

"I've heard a lot about you, as well," Jenny replied.

"Don't you believe one word of it," Chuck retorted.

"It's all been good," she quickly assured him.

"That's what I mean. Don't you believe one word of it."

"My dad has a unique sense of humor," Rafe inserted dryly.

"Grandpa knows lots'n'lots'a jokes," Cindy stated. "Tell her the one about the naked lady, Grandpa!"

"Some other time, half-pint," Chuck said, ruffling her hair with one of his huge hamlike hands.

"I know it by heart!" Cindy proudly proclaimed. "I can say it. Did you hear the one about the naked lady who—"

Rafe hurriedly clapped his hand over his daughter's mouth before she could go into greater detail with one of his father's slightly off-color jokes, as old as the sea itself. Rafe distracted Cindy by picking her up in one arm. "Let's go eat, kiddo. I'm hungry enough to gobble you right up." Hauling his daughter higher, he nibbled on her neck, removing his hand from her mouth as girlish shrieks filled the air.

"Such merriment is not good for the digestion," Hugo declared disapprovingly.

"Don't sweat it, Hughie," Spud advised with a pat to the chef's thin shoulder. "The kid's got a cast-iron stomach."

Hugo didn't say a word, letting his sniff communicate his disdain.

"Don't mind him." Spud's aside was directed toward Jenny. "He always has his shorts in a twist over something."

Jenny tried to hide her smile as she followed the others into a room off the front of the kitchen. "This used to be the kitchen of the original house," Rafe noted as he seated her. "When we redid the place, we added the brand-new commercial kitchen out back and turned this room into a dining room for us. Makes it easy to eat and sample the wares."

Jenny nodded, appreciating the advantages to be had from living right above a great restaurant. Had Rafe not insisted on taking her home with him, she'd have been staring at a frozen dinner about now, had she eaten at all.

"You know what, Grandpa? Jenny makes teddy bears," Cindy piped up from across the table.

Hugo sniffed his telltale sign of disapproval as he deposited a tureen full of soup on the table. "Potage," he announced before regally sailing out again.

"His fancy way of saying soup. It's celery-and-walnut soup," Spud said as he ladled out the portions into individual soup bowls. "Sounds weird but tastes okay, like most of Hughie's cooking."

During the meal, the conversation ebbed and flowed around Jenny without forcing her to participate, for which she was grateful. She was so tired that it took all the energy she had to concentrate on eating. She wasn't sure she could have formed coherent sentences, as well, at that point.

After the big meal topped off with a generous helping of pineapple upside-down cake, Jenny felt like a new woman. Which was a good thing because there was no holding Cindy down any longer. She was practically bursting with excitement as she tugged Jenny upstairs with her, eager to show off her room and her toys, not to mention the major production of getting her nails polished.

The little girl talked a mile a minute and moved around the room like a whirling dervish. It was a perfect little girl's room, complete with a canopied bed in pink-and-white eyelet. Cindy's toys were surprisingly eclectic, ranging from a favorite baby doll to a race-car track complete with garage and gas station. Once Jenny had been given the complete tour, they sat on Cindy's twin bed with the makeup kit spread out before them.

"Here, put your hand on my leg," Jenny said, figuring it would be easier to paint a target that wasn't moving the way Cindy's fingers had a tendency to do as she pointed out yet another treasure in her room. "Okay, now keep them there while I paint your nails, okay?"

The little girl nodded, biting her bottom lip with anticipation as she watched Jenny with the intense concentration of an intern watching brain surgery being performed.

Once the nails on Cindy's left hand were done, in Bubblegum Pink, Jenny said, "Okay, let's switch hands. Put your other hand here but don't touch anything with your other hand yet because the polish is still wet."

Cindy obligingly put her hand in the air and then rested her head trustingly against Jenny's side as she completed the polish job. The gesture brought a lump to Jenny's throat.

"Are you gonna stay over tonight?" Cindy asked her. "We could have a sleepover and talk all night."

"That would be fun, but I have to go home."

"How come?"

"Because my teddy bears would be lonely there all by themselves," Jenny said, relieved she came up with something the little girl could probably relate to. Telling Cindy that she couldn't stay because of the way Rafe made her feel wouldn't have done at all.

As if conjured up by her thoughts, Rafe appeared in the doorway. "You two done in here yet? It's past your bathtime, kiddo. And then it's time for bed."

"Look, Daddy!" Cindy exclaimed, bouncing off the bed and rushing over to her father to show off her pink nails. "Aren't they... impressive?"

Rafe grinned at the use of his daughter's now-favorite word. "Very impressive, pumpkin."

"You'll stay until I go to bed, right?" Cindy turned to ask Jenny, who nodded.

The bathroom was close enough down the hallway that Jenny could hear the water running and the giggles of the little girl as she took her bath. In no time at all, both father and daughter were back—she in her flowered pajamas and he slightly damp from their play as Cindy rode piggyback on her father's back. Once around the room and then Cindy was dumped on the bed at Jenny's side.

"Where's my storybook, Daddy?" Cindy demanded once she was right side up again.

"In the living room. Let's read another story tonight."

"No. We have to read *Sleeping Beauty*."

"You've heard that one twenty times, kiddo."

"I know. It's my favorite. I don't like Grandpa's fish story."

"*Moby Dick*," Rafe told Jenny. "It's Pop's favorite book. Okay, kiddo. You wait here and I'll go get *Sleeping Beauty* for you."

"You want to brush my hair?" Cindy asked Jenny once her father was gone.

Jenny nodded and took the brush the little girl had picked up from the bedside table. "I wish my hair was nice like yours," Cindy said wistfully as Jenny began brushing.

"Your hair *is* nice," Jenny assured her. "You have beautiful curly hair."

"It gets in knots and it's hard to brush. Then Grandpa swears. Sometimes I get three dimes when he brushes my hair."

"Men aren't always good at things like brushing hair," Jenny acknowledged with a rueful grin.

"My daddy is good at it. Almost as good as you are."

"You're very lucky to have such a good daddy."

"My daddy is the best daddy in the whole world," Cindy proudly proclaimed.

Swallowing the sudden knot in her throat, Jenny nodded her agreement.

"Here you go, kiddo." Rafe was back and held the book up for her to see. *"Sleeping Beauty."*

Cindy insisted on Jenny reading all the princess's parts.

"Aren't you gonna wake her with a kiss, Daddy?"

Jenny froze. After the monster day she'd had, she didn't think she had the defenses left to keep Rafe at arm's length if he kissed her.

"Not tonight, kiddo," Rafe replied. "Sleeping Beauty didn't have an audience when she got that kiss. Time for lights out."

Cindy threw her arms around Jenny's neck before lying back down and snuggling into her pillow.

"I started some coffee. Decaf," Rafe told Jenny as they stood in the hallway outside his daughter's room. "Would you like a cup?"

Jenny nodded.

"It's all ready. Just help yourself." Rafe gestured toward the living room. "Kitchen, such as it is, is off to the left. The cups are in the cupboard above the sink," he added. "I've got to go downstairs and check on things. Spud and Hugo were yelling the place down a while ago. I won't be gone long."

His absence gave Jenny a chance to look around the living room on her own. The walls and rug were a neutral beige. Splashes of color were provided by the blue throw pillows on the couch, which matched the colors in the oil painting of a stormy sea above the fireplace.

The kitchen area was an efficiency-size area just off the living room and the coffee was ready to be poured from the coffeemaker by the time Jenny entered. With cup in hand, she headed back to a winged armchair to wait for Rafe's return.

She'd no sooner sat down than a gray-and-white cat jumped onto her lap. "Boots, I presume," Jenny noted wryly.

The cat circled three times before settling down and making herself at home, her greeny-yellow eyes closing as she started purring. Unable to resist, Jenny put her cup on the end table and started petting Boots. Rubbing the cat's gray ears made the purring double in intensity.

"Looks like you've found a friend," Rafe said as he rejoined Jenny.

"She found me."

"Cats have a way of doing that," Rafe acknowledged.

Jenny nodded, looking down at the contented cat and feeling that all-too-familiar lump in her throat. Her emotions seemed to be on the verge of getting the better of her tonight.

Must be exhaustion setting in, she decided. It was stupid to sit there and feel teary-eyed just because she had a cat on her lap—yet another thing she'd longed for and hadn't gotten as a little girl.

Apparently sensing something was wrong, Rafe said, "If the cat is bothering you, just shoo her down."

"No, the cat is fine. I was just thinking . . . remembering how I'd always wanted a cat when I was a kid. But I lived with my grandparents and my grandfather hated cats."

"What about now?"

"Now?"

"You're on your own. You could have a cat now if you wanted to."

"I know. And I plan on doing that as soon as things settle down a bit."

"Well, if you feel the need for feline company until you get a cat of your own, you're welcome to come over and spend some time petting Boots if you'd like."

"Thanks."

"Of course it goes without saying that you're also welcome to come over and spend time with me anytime you'd like, as well. Pet me, too, if you want."

"How generous of you," she returned in the same mocking tone he'd used.

"So, Jenny, tell me—why teddy bears?"

She smiled, relieved that he was moving the conversation onto a less intimate subject. This was a question she knew the answer to. The truth was that her dad may have taken off, and her mother died, but her teddy bear had been the one constant in her young life.

Aloud, she simply said, "I've loved teddy bears since I was a kid. My grandmother taught me how to sew and I made clothes for my bear out of remnant scraps of material. Then I started making a new bear of my own, since we couldn't afford to buy a new one. It was a pitiful attempt— I was only ten. But I got better with practice, and by using and adapting some patterns I found in library books. By the time I was a teenager, I was making a few bears for my friends. The bears were popular and soon other people wanted me to make bears for them, as well. But it wasn't until I happened to read an article in a collector's magazine that I realized that there might actually be a larger market for my talent. That was six years ago, when I was a junior in college."

Jenny took a sip of her coffee before continuing. "Of course, I'm too practical to not have something to fall back on, so I got my degree in business administration with a minor in art. When I graduated, I worked for two years in the personnel department of a large insurance company. All the while, I kept making bears in my spare time and selling them at some of the regional teddy-bear shows on the weekends. I also spent a lot of time at the library researching bear collecting. That's when I discovered doll- and teddy-bear collecting was the third-most popular kind of collecting in this country. Only stamps and coins were ahead of them. Almost four years ago I made enough selling my teddy bears to quit my job and strike out on my own." Feeling that she'd been talking about herself for too long, Jenny said, "But enough about me. What about you?"

"What about me?" he said.

"You're very good with Cindy," Jenny told him.

"My mother-in-law wouldn't agree with you," Rafe retorted. "She's been very vocal lately in her disapproval of the way I'm raising Cindy."

"What could she possibly disapprove of?" Jenny countered.

"The lack of 'feminine' influences in my daughter's life. She's got a point. Cindy lives in an all-male household here. You saw how excited she got about a little thing like you doing her nails for her."

"Cindy herself told me that she's got the best daddy in the world, and I'd have to say that I agree with her."

"I appreciate the vote of confidence," he said.

"Anytime."

Her eyes got caught by the warmth in his. For the first time, it was a friendly warmth, not just a sensual one. The result was doubly tempting, creating a bridge between them. It was one of those moments in time that you'd look back on and say something special happened here. A special kind of bond was being formed between them, but it was disrupted by Boots the cat suddenly jumping down from Jenny's lap.

Looking away from his magnetic gaze, Jenny murmured, "It's getting late. I should be going."

"I'll walk you home," Rafe replied.

To her surprise, when they got to her front porch, he merely smoothed a loose strand of her hair behind her ear and kissed her chastely on her forehead before turning to leave, with instructions for her to be sure and lock her door.

She put out a hand to stop him. "Wait a second. I've been meaning to give you something...."

His grin was wolfish in the darkness. "You have?" His voice was filled with anticipation.

"Wait here a second."

She was back in no time. "Here." She handed him Bruiser, newly repaired. "I hope you don't mind that I put a sweater on him. There was a section up near his shoulder that I wasn't able to repair, so I left it as it was, but I thought the sweater covered the area nicely. What do you think?"

"That I should never jump to conclusions where you're concerned," Rafe replied ruefully. "Good night."

Jenny slept like a log that night. She was awakened first thing Monday morning by a phone call from her insurance adjuster. She'd barely gotten showered and dressed when she got another call. "Hello?"

"Leave," a muffled male voice said.

Jenny immediately hung up the phone. She no longer thought the call was a crank. Now she took it seriously. Someone was clearly sending her a message here. The question was: who?

The phone rang again. She let her answering machine screen the call, which this time was from the bank manager, Mr. Friendall. Jenny picked up the receiver to speak to him.

"Would it be possible for you to drop by my office this morning?" Mr. Friendall said. "We need to discuss some matters that I'd really rather not go into over the phone."

Naturally, after a comment like that, Jenny agreed to come right over, her worries about the threatening phone call put on the back burner in favor of worries about what the bank might want. Miriam promised to deal with the insurance adjuster while Jenny hotfooted it over to the bank.

To give Mr. Friendall his due, he cut right to the chase after a minimum of rambling. The bottom line was that the bank, having recently been taken over by another, had reviewed her loan and found it too "risky" so they were stopping her line of credit.

Not the best way to begin a new work week, Jenny thought somewhat hysterically as she stepped out into the sunshine. First the sabotage, then the flood and now this! Someone was pretty determined that she not succeed with Benjamin Bear and Company. And while it might be convenient to blame Rafe, she'd seen the look on his face when he'd followed her into the barn last night. He'd been as stunned as she was.

No, there was something else going on here and she was going to find out what it was. Her first stop was the library, where she did a bit of research on the new ownership of the bank. "Bingo!" she exclaimed, earning her a frown from the reference librarian.

There it was, in black and white. The same conglomerate that owned the bank also owned MegaToys—the company that wanted her to sell them her designs. The company that hadn't taken her refusal lightly.

Suddenly the puzzle fell into place. The anonymous phone calls, the missing sketches, the lost shipments, the construction delays, the mysterious leak in the roof, which Mr. Fadden had told her he suspected had been made deliberately. And now her line of credit being stopped. Everything led right to MegaToys' doorstep! Not enough so for her to take any kind of legal action, but enough for her to be convinced that MegaToys was behind it all.

Finding herself in this sudden cash crunch, Jenny thought longingly of the trust fund her grandmother had left her. That seventy thousand dollars would come in very handy right now. In fact, it was vital that she have it—given this latest development with the bank. The problem was that the inheritance was intended to be an old-fashioned "dowry" and came with strings regarding Jenny being married. But had her grandmother known of the dire straits in which she currently found herself, Jenny was sure she'd approve of her gaining access to the money now.

Therefore, her next order of business was to call her attorney. "Listen, Miranda, I need to talk to you about my grandmother's will."

"What about it?"

"How long would it take to break it? To delete that clause that says I have to be married before I can get my inheritance?"

"It would take several weeks at a minimum," Miriam replied. "Why? I thought you were happy leaving the money in the mutual funds where it is. It's been earning a great rate of return for you. Why bring this up now?"

"Because the bank is putting the screws on me. They've stopped my line of credit, claiming I'm too risky. Told me this morning that they've reevaluated my loan and decided that it has to be paid up in full. I did a little checking on my own and found out that it just so happens that the bank is owned by the same conglomerate that owns MegaToys."

"The toy company that's been after you for your designs?"

"*After me* is putting it mildly! They were highly insulted when I turned down their offer. I explained that I wanted the bears to be well made and that their company had a reputation for shoddy workmanship. They use inferior material, use work-camp labor and then gouge the customer, pocketing big revenues."

"Welcome to business in the nineties," Miranda stated.

"Not *my* business," Jenny retorted.

"I hate to be the voice of gloom here, but even if we got that clause of your grandmother's will overturned, the other clause would still stand about you not receiving the money until you're thirty. As it stands now it's until you're thirty *or* until you marry, whichever comes first."

Jenny frowned. "So you're saying that there's no way I can have access to that money now?"

"No. Not unless you get married. And the will also stipulates that you can't use it as collateral for a loan."

"I know. That's why I went to the bank in the first place. And they were great. But only a few weeks later they were taken over by another bank. You know how local banks are going under all over the place. I didn't take any notice of it until I got a phone call this morning requesting a meeting ASAP."

"I'm sorry I don't have any better answers for you. How quickly do they want the money?"

"Yesterday," Jenny noted wryly. "How quickly could I get the money if I *did* get married?"

"A matter of days once I set things in motion. Why? Are you planning on tying the knot?"

"Looks like I might have to," Jenny muttered. "Whether I want to or not."

"A few rooms above a bar is no place to bring up a young lady," Rafe's mother-in-law, Althea Layton, icily stated over the phone.

Rafe could have told her that Murphy's wasn't a bar, it was a restaurant. And that they didn't live in a few rooms, it was the entire top two floors of the house. But his mother-in-law already knew that. It made no difference. Her disapproval was unrelenting. So all he said was, "We've had this argument before."

"Yes, we have. Do you realize that Cindy actually told me an obscene joke today? Is that how you're raising her? To tell dirty jokes?"

"She doesn't tell dirty jokes."

"In my opinion, she does."

"A little off-color maybe...."

"I suppose it depends on your taste. If you were raised with riffraff, perhaps you might call it off-color. But Susan wouldn't have called it off-color, and you know it. My poor daughter would be distraught at the way her only child's upbringing is being handled. Or mishandled.''

"Listen, you've got no right telling me how to raise my daughter,'' Rafe retorted angrily, her comments about Susan having hit home. "You never even bothered to see her until she was three.''

"I was too distraught over my daughter's death. I was overcome with grief.''

"You were too wrapped up in your own life to give a damn!''

"There you go, swearing again. I told my daughter no good would come of marrying you and I was right. Look where she ended up. Dead.''

"I didn't kill her." Rafe gritted the words between clenched teeth. "She died of leukemia.''

"If she hadn't been so run down from trying to help you set up that stupid bar of yours, she wouldn't have gotten sick in the first place.''

This was another argument they'd had, going back even further than the one about Cindy's upbringing. Rafe had lived with the guilt long enough. "This conversation is over,'' he stated.

"Yes, it is,'' his mother-in-law agreed. "The next communication will be from my attorney.''

"Your attorney?''

"That's right. I'm going to file suit to get custody of my only granddaughter.'' With that bit of news, she hung up.

"You look the way I feel,'' Rafe told Jenny as he sat waiting for her on the top step of her front porch.

"And how's that?''

"Rotten.''

"There you go, sweet-talking me again,'' she noted, but her voice held more weariness than mockery as she sat beside him.

"Yeah, right.'' He sounded as depressed as she felt.

"I've had an incredibly bad day," Jenny acknowledged. "How about you?"

"I've got the mother-in-law from hell breathing down my neck just itching to take my daughter away from me," Rafe declared.

Jenny was so surprised that she temporarily forgot her own troubles. "You're kidding me."

"I wish I were, believe me."

"But why on earth would she want to take Cindy away from you?"

"You remember that talk you and I had the other night? About me worrying that Cindy didn't have many feminine influences in her life?"

Jenny nodded.

"My mother-in-law feels Cindy needs a feminine role model. Herself. So she's threatening to file suit in order to get custody of Cindy herself."

"Could she do that? Surely no court would take Cindy away from you."

"I don't aim to find out. There's no way I'm going to put my daughter through a dirty custody battle. While Susan's mother most likely wouldn't win, she has the money at her disposal to make things very difficult, to draw things out in the court."

"So what are you going to do?"

"I've thought about it and the bottom line is that I need a wife in order to keep my daughter. The sooner the better. I don't suppose you'd be interested in the job, would you?"

"You know, it's funny you should mention it," Jenny said, "because it just so happens that I need a husband. Pronto!"

Chapter Five

"**Y**ou want to run that past me again?" Rafe said slowly, as if unable to believe his luck.

"I need a husband."

"Why?"

"Business reasons." Jenny rather liked the sound of that. It certainly wasn't as crass as saying "For the money."

"Would you care to elaborate on that?" Rafe inquired.

"My grandmother left me a substantial sum of money that unfortunately I can't gain access to until I'm thirty...or married. Whichever comes first."

"I thought you said your family wasn't wealthy."

"They weren't. My grandmother received this money as a settlement from the hospital where my grandfather died. There was negligence involved. Anyway, my grandmother refused to touch a penny of it. She said it would be like celebrating his death. She put it into an investment account and left it to me in her will."

"With stipulations."

Jenny nodded. "There's very little in life that doesn't come with stipulations."

"Have you consulted an attorney about this?"

Again, she nodded. "When my grandmother first died four years ago, I consulted my attorney once I discovered the details of the will. The marriage stipulation wouldn't be that difficult to turn over, but the 'age thirty' clause would be trickier. However, at that time I didn't want to take it to court—that seemed too much like going against my grandmother's wishes, and I didn't want to do that. She intended that money to be a dowry for me. I was used to making it on my own. I didn't *really* need the money before."

"And now?"

"It's imperative that I have the money for my company, but I can't afford the time delay a long legal procedure would cause. I only have a limited window of opportunity here and a certain large corporation would like to see that window closed. They don't want to see me succeed with Benjamin Bear and Company."

"Why not?"

"Because MegaToys wants my designs for themselves. When I refused to sell, they decided to make my life difficult. They were the ones behind the delayed shipments and the other acts of sabotage, including the roof. I'm sure of it. Mr. Fadden told me that he suspected someone made that hole in the roof deliberately."

"Why didn't you tell me about this last night? Did you think I was the one who'd done it?"

"No. Not when I saw your face yesterday after you followed me to the barn. You were as surprised as I was. And the reason I didn't talk about it last night is that I was too worn-out."

"You still look worn-out," he noted with some concern.

She bumped against him in teasing chastisement. "Enough with the compliments already."

Rafe smiled for a moment and Jenny felt as if the sun had come out from behind the clouds. But moments later his brooding look was back, along with a large dose of skepticism. "You really think a toy company would go to those kinds of extremes over a few teddy bears?"

"Collecting antique bears and manufacturing new ones is a trillion-dollar, international business," Jenny countered. "You bet I believe the toy company is behind it! Peter Vanborne, the president of the company, has a reputation for getting what he wants."

"So do I. That doesn't mean I'd break the law to get it."

"This guy would. Vanborne has a reputation for shady business dealings, but he makes the shareholders money, so no one cares. He's a real *gonif*, which is why I didn't want anything to do with him or his company."

"*Gonif?*" Rafe repeated in confusion.

"One of Miriam's expressions. It means he's a crook. I'll bet he's behind those menacing phone calls I got, not to mention the fact that he actually had the nerve to have someone snooping around in my house—"

"Wait a second here," Rafe interrupted her. "What are you talking about? When did they get into your house?"

"You remember that afternoon we went on our picnic?"

Rafe nodded, not likely to forget that day—the first time he'd kissed her, the first time he'd known for sure that something was going on between them.

"Well, later that evening I was kind of restless...." Jenny blushed and hurried on. "Anyway, I decided to work on some designs for some new Bambino bears, but I couldn't because the sketches were gone. I looked high and low but there was no sign of them."

"Maybe you just misplaced them."

"That's what I thought at the time, but there were other things out of place, as well. Although I didn't know it at the time, someone must have been in my house and taken those sketches."

"That does it. You need more protection, starting with a top-notch security system, the kind that will contact the police for you. One for the barn, one for your house. What if you'd gotten home earlier and caught them still in your house? You should have called the police right away."

"And said what? That I'd lost some teddy-bear sketches? You didn't believe me, either, when I just told you."

"Yeah, well if those jerks try any more funny business, they'll have to deal with me," Rafe growled. "Because from now on, if someone messes with you, they'll answer to me. You've got someone looking after you from here on out."

Red flags went up in Jenny's mind. She'd had men make rash promises like that before. And they never stayed around long enough to keep them. Her father had promised her that he'd take care of her, yet he'd taken off when she was six. She'd spent years secretly waiting for him to come back. He never had. She'd only discovered a few years ago that he'd moved to Florida and started another family there before dying of a heart attack at the age of fifty. End of story.

The moral was that men said things they didn't mean. She knew that. She also knew that the best way to protect herself was to look out for herself. "I'm not in the market for a real husband," she warned Rafe.

"And I'm not in the market for a real wife," Rafe concurred. "This would be a practical arrangement."

"For me, too," she immediately agreed, telling herself that his words should have reassured her. So why didn't they?

"Have you ever been married before?" Rafe asked her.

Jenny shook her head.

"Do you have some guy waiting in the wings?"

"If I did, would I be agreeing to this idea?" she countered in exasperation. "Look, *you* love your daughter. *I* love my company. I'm going to fight to protect it the same way you're fighting to keep and protect your daughter."

"I'm not talking about a short-term deal here," Rafe warned her. "I don't want Cindy upset by having you walk out of our arrangement next week, next month or next year."

"I'd never do anything to hurt Cindy."

"A minimum term of five years, optional to be renewed after that time," Rafe stated.

Jenny reflected back on how quickly the past five years had gone by. She'd been busy getting involved in bear making and setting up her business. And then she looked ahead to the plans she had—a five-year plan laid out for her company. Plenty to do. Plenty to keep her busy. Five years might seem like a long time to some people, but it didn't seem that long to her.

Besides she cared about Cindy and certainly didn't want to see her hurt. And she didn't want to see her involved in a custody battle. She knew firsthand how good a parent Rafe was, acting as both mother and father to his daughter.

As if sensing her thoughts, Rafe softly murmured, "I think you'd be a good mother to Cindy."

"Would that be okay with you? I mean, I wouldn't dream of trying to take her real mother's place. I mean, I wouldn't be able to even if I wanted to. I mean..." Her tongue seemed tied in knots as she futilely strove to express herself.

"I know what you mean," Rafe assured her.

Taking a deep breath, Jenny said, "If we're really going to do this, there are a few things I need to clarify. Umm, I don't know quite how to put this...."

"Just say it."

"I just have to make sure that this isn't an elaborate way for you to get your hands on my property," she blurted out. "I mean, you haven't exactly hidden the fact that you wanted to expand your restaurant and you need this land to do that."

Rafe stiffened, his face etched with angry impatience. "My daughter is more important to me than a hundred res-

taurants!" he growled. "But to prove it to you, I'll have my
attorney draw up an agreement that this damn land re-
mains yours. Does that make you happy?"

"Don't bite my head off," Jenny retorted. "It was a valid
question given the circumstances."

"Any more questions?" he demanded.

"As a matter of fact, yes. Are you proposing a marriage
in name only?" she asked him, irritation making her more
direct than normal.

"Not necessarily, no."

"But you said you didn't need a real wife," she reminded him, wondering if what she was experiencing was
fear or anticipation, or a mixture of both.

"I meant a wife in the traditional sense," Rafe clarified.
"I mean, this isn't exactly a traditional setup here. We each
have personal reasons for getting married. We've both been
up-front about those reasons. The things we love most in the
world are being threatened. So we're making moves to protect what's ours."

"Right," Jenny agreed.

"But that doesn't mean that we have to deny the chem-
istry that's between us," Rafe added.

"So what are you saying?" she asked cautiously.

"That we should just play this by ear. Five years is a long
time to go without any kind of physical relationship. And I
don't believe in playing around."

"I don't, either," she quickly concurred.

"See? We share a lot already. We share a similar sense of
humor, a similar sense of values. We've developed a friendship. And there's no denying the sexual attraction. It could
be the basis for a good relationship."

She noticed how carefully Rafe avoided using the word
love, not that she could blame him. After all, he'd been
married before to a woman he had obviously loved very
deeply. She couldn't blame him for looking for something
different this time around.

She wasn't looking for love, either, Jenny firmly reminded herself. Whenever men said they loved her, they took off—starting with her father. She'd learned at an early age that you couldn't trust men to be there when you needed them, and nothing she'd experienced since those childhood days had done anything to change her mind. If anything, her experiences as an adult had only reconfirmed her belief that when the going got tough, the supposedly tough took off.

Jenny realized that not all men were like her father, that not all men abandoned their families. But deep down she secretly wondered if there wasn't something about *her* that drove men away, made them leave. This way—with the ending built into this relationship with Rafe—she knew up front that he'd be leaving and even knew when.

That's why this arrangement of a marriage of convenience between them made sense. Avoid love and you avoided hassles and disappointment. Rafe wasn't offering her love. He was offering to make her part of his family for a certain period of time, offering to have her participate in his daughter's upbringing. In exchange for which she got what she wanted—Benjamin Bear and Company and the money she needed for its survival. It wasn't the way she would have scripted things, but it made for a livable compromise.

She couldn't afford to fool herself for a minute here. No self-delusions. She had to be very clear about the fact that Rafe wasn't claiming to love her. She knew he didn't want to love anyone ever again. He didn't have to tell her that. It didn't take a mind reader to figure out that his wife's death had put him through the wringer. She'd picked up that much from one or two of the comments his dad had made when she'd gone over for dinner last night.

"I can promise you that I won't do anything you don't want me to do," Rafe said into the silence that had grown between them.

"You're a man who always goes after what he wants," Jenny stated.

"I won't deny that. But as much as I might want you, I want my daughter to grow up in a stable household even more."

He couldn't make it clearer than that, Jenny thought to herself, telling herself that funny pang in her chest was caused by hunger. She'd skipped breakfast and lunch.

"So what do you say?" Rafe asked.

"I say yes," Jenny replied.

Like the partners they were about to become, they shook on it. To Jenny, it just seemed like the right thing to do. She wasn't nearly so sure about the rightness or correctness of the insidious warmth originating from his fingers clasping hers. She'd hoped that the practical discussion they'd just had about their marriage would have gone a long way toward diluting her sensually charged reaction to his touch. So far, no such luck.

Tugging her hand away, she briskly said, "So when do we get married?"

"The sooner, the better."

"I agree."

"Okay, what do you say to ten days from now? It will take a week to get the blood tests and license sorted out let alone getting things set up."

"What kinds of things?" Jenny asked, never having been part of planning a wedding before, let alone her own.

"Witnesses, a small reception afterward—that sort of thing. We don't want it to look like we're getting married in too much of a hurry or that will raise suspicions. This has to look like a real marriage to everyone else, or the plan will fall through. If Althea—that's my mother-in-law—if she sniffs a setup, she'll go ahead and file that custody suit anyway."

"She won't smell a thing, but a bed of roses," Jenny retorted, disliking the other woman intensely already. "Are you going to invite her to the ceremony?"

"No. I'll send her an announcement after the fact. I wouldn't put it past her to try and make a scene otherwise."

"She sounds like a real winner," Jenny muttered.

Rafe nodded his agreement. "I find it hard to believe she could have had a daughter as sweet as Susan was."

There it was, Jenny noted. That melancholy look in his eyes whenever he mentioned or thought of his wife. It was a look she wanted to erase. "So," she said with false bravado, "when do we break the news?"

"No time like the present. Let's go home and tell Cindy and my dad now."

"Now? *Right* now?"

"Something wrong with that?"

"No, it's just that I only met your dad for the first time last night. I hope he doesn't think it's strange for us to be announcing our engagement one day later."

"No stranger than us getting married in ten days," Rafe pointed out. "Trust me, Pop will be delighted. He liked you. Besides, he's the spontaneous type. He won't think it's strange at all."

"What about Cindy?"

"She'll be delighted. She wanted you to move in last night. She told me so after her bath."

"Maybe that's just because I'm the unusual stranger who lives next door and makes teddy bears. Once I move in, she might not think I'm so neat."

"Why not?"

Jenny shrugged.

"Your dad did a pretty good job on your self-esteem, didn't he?" Rafe noted astutely.

"I barely remember my father at all," Jenny replied.

"Maybe not, but I'm willing to bet that you remember the pain he caused you very well."

Shrugging again, she looked away, dislodging her hair in the process so that several strands slid forward, partially shielding her face from view. "I'm used to making it on my own," she maintained.

"That's all very well and good, but you don't have to make it on your own anymore," he softly returned, tucking the wayward strands of hair behind her ear as he'd done last night.

"I'm not looking for a father figure," Jenny told him.

"And I can assure you my feelings toward you aren't at all paternal," he assured her with a wolfish grin. "So come on, let's go break the news and face the music." He held out his hand to her.

Jenny paused a moment. This was it. Did she really have what it took to go through with this plan? As Miriam would say, Jenny would need plenty of moxie in order to see this one through.

Jenny had never been known in the past for her moxie. In fact, her grandfather had constantly accused her of being too soft, too emotional. He'd warned her that no one succeeded in this life without plenty of determination and tenacity. Jenny looked at Rafe. Yeah, spending the next five years with a man this easy on the eyes is gonna require a lot of determination and tenacity, she could practically hear Miriam saying. A tough job, but someone's gotta do it. Her decision made, Jenny grinned and took Rafe's hand.

Waiting for the laughter to die down after Spud's latest outrageous toast to the engaged couple, Hugo sniffed his disapproval. Watching Spud down his glassful of champagne in one go, Hugo said, "You have the soul of a peasant."

"So you've told me," Spud returned, patting Hugo on the back with such force, the wiry chef almost bent over double. "At least once a day. You've gotta come up with something new, Hughie. You're starting to sound like a broken record."

Hugo let forth a virulent spew of French.

Spud cracked up. "You forget, Hughie. I was born up in the North Country, near the border with French-Canadian Quebec so I understood every garbled word of that. But I suppose for a boy born in the South Bronx, you didn't sound too bad. Got most of the accents right."

"Malicious lies. I have never been to the South Bronx!"

"That's not what I hear," Spud taunted him.

Infuriated, Hugo spun around, only to have his tall chef's hat knock one of his precious copper saucepans from its hanger above the stove onto the floor. "Now look what you've made me do!" Hugo wailed, before snatching up the empty saucepan and clasping it to his heaving chest. "There is no room in this kitchen! An artist needs more room!"

"Listen, you two, this is supposed to be a celebration here, not the beginning of another battle of the chefs," Rafe warned.

Hugo straightened his lopsided chef's hat with the haughtiness of a king straightening his royal crown. "There is only one chef in this kitchen," Hugo proclaimed.

"That's right," Spud agreed. "And you're looking at him," he added, thumping himself on his chest.

"You two are going to make Jenny regret her decision to join this family," Chuck mockingly noted.

"You won't change your mind, will you, Jenny?" Cindy asked in dismay.

"No, I won't change my mind," Jenny reassured her, adding a hug for extra measure.

"Good." Cindy beamed. "Then you can live here and paint my nails all the time."

"I'm sure Jenny is looking forward to that with bated breath," Chuck inserted with a grin. "But we can't waste time standing around here. We've got calls to make, invitations to get out."

"It's going to be a small wedding ceremony, Pop," Rafe reminded his dad. "Small reception, too. So don't go overboard here."

"I served for over thirty years in the navy, son," Chuck retorted. "I think I know how to avoid going overboard."

Famous last words...

"What happened to a small ceremony at city hall?" Jenny muttered ten days later as she sat beside Miriam in a white stretch limousine complete with leather seats and a mini-bar.

"Hall-schmall," Miriam retorted with no sympathy whatsoever. "That was a cockamamie idea in the first place. Besides, Max and the judge have been buddies for years. Since you refused to be married in a church, this was the next best thing. It's only right that you be married in his chambers."

"The churches were all booked on such short notice," Jenny reminded her. "We would have had to wait until December."

"I told you I have a few connections...."

"No. This is fine, Miriam. Really." What Jenny didn't say was that Rafe and Susan had been married in a large church service, complete with four bridesmaids. She'd seen the photograph when she'd moved some of her things over to Rafe's house. She hadn't been trying to pry. She'd been looking for an empty drawer. Instead she'd found the picture. Captured there forever was the way Rafe looked at Susan, as if the sun rose and set with her. With trembling fingers, Jenny had replaced the photo exactly where she'd found it. A church wedding would only remind Rafe of what he'd lost. But she couldn't tell Miriam that.

Jenny also hadn't told Miriam about the practical nature of this arrangement with Rafe. It had been tough not spilling the beans to Miriam who was, after all, Jenny's closest friend. But Jenny realized it was probably for the best that she was honoring Rafe's request that they keep the truth to themselves. And the bottom line was that she did feel a teensy bit guilty for marrying for money. But she was marrying for her *own* money, not his, Jenny reminded herself. Surely she wouldn't be struck down by lightning for that?

"So are there any questions you want to ask me during these last few minutes before you become a married woman?" Miriam turned in the soft leather seat to inquire with a grin.

"Yes. Can we turn the car around and go back home?"

"Ah, wedding jitters. I was wondering when you'd get around to having them."

"Jitters? Is that what you call these two-story-high dinosaurs in my stomach?"

"If I ate the breakfast you did, I'd have two-story-high dinosaurs in my stomach, too," Miriam retorted.

"I needed calming down."

"So you ate half a jar of chocolate frosting, straight from the can."

"It's always worked in the past when I was nervous about something. I feel sick. I haven't gotten a good night's sleep since I got engaged and it's not what you think," she added with a dark look in Miriam's direction.

"Stop with your *kvetching*, already," Miriam told her with a grin. "You know you want to marry Rafe. I knew it, too, the first time I saw you two together."

"You know, most friends would think it was a little strange that we were getting married so quickly," Jenny retorted grumpily. "You could have at least tried to talk me out of it or something. Advised caution."

"Caution you've got plenty of," Miriam stated, her grin getting even wider. "I don't have to give you caution. Good advice—now this I can give you lots of."

"So what's your good advice?"

"Go for it. And remember what I told you about Max and me. I knew he was the one the first time we met."

"Must be nice to be so sure about things," Jenny noted.

"Who said anything about being sure? We didn't know how things would work out. But we had faith and that can get you through just about anything. Remember that and you'll do just fine."

Miriam's hug made Jenny feel better. "Thanks for being such a wonderful friend, Miriam. And for agreeing to be my matron of honor and listening to all my *kvetching*. I don't know what I'd have done without you."

Blinking away tears, Miriam said, "Enough already, you're going to crush my new chapeau. You haven't said what you think of it? There a reason for that?"

"It's a gorgeous hat. I like all the ribbons and flowers."

"Max said it was a *mishmash* of a hat. I told him, 'This coming from a man who can't pick out a tie and matching shirt in the morning?' He decided he liked my hat after all."

"Wise man," Jenny noted.

"That's one of the reasons I married him," Miriam said. "Because he is so wise. You know I gave Rafe a few words to the wise, as well."

"You did?"

"Certainly. I told him a few of the rules for a successful marriage that I keep stuck on the refrigerator door. Rule number one—the female *always* makes the rules. Rule number two—the rules are subject to change at any time without prior notification. And Rule number three is that no male can possibly know all the rules. But my favorite is number five, which is that the female is *never* wrong."

Jenny cracked up. "What did Rafe say?"

"He reacted the same way you did. He laughed. I told you he was a *mensch*. You two will be good for each other, help each other heal."

There was no more time for conversation as the limo smoothly pulled in front of the courthouse. The building, red brick with white trimming, looked like something right out of a Norman Rockwell painting. Rafe, on the other hand, looked liked something out of *GQ*. He stood waiting for her near the curb, wearing a perfectly tailored navy blue suit and a snowy white shirt with a burgundy tie.

She wondered what he'd think of her choice of dress. Actually it was a white suit, classy and elegant with the only touch of color being the light blue silk blouse she wore with it. The blouse's V neck was the perfect foil for the suit's collarless jacket. The skirt's hem swirled midcalf.

She'd had her hair done into a chignon and had the hairstylist tuck in a sprig or two of baby's breath. The stylist had also done her makeup, using a palette of color to bring out the blue in Jenny's eyes and the rosy curve of her lips. She'd even had a manicure, a first for her. Jenny had been pleased with the results. She hoped Rafe was, too.

All he said was "Thank goodness you're here. Cindy has been driving us nuts, wondering when you're going to arrive."

So much for Rafe noticing her, Jenny thought with self-deprecating humor. "Where is she?"

"Inside with Pop. I suspect he's trying to teach her how to play poker."

"I can see I'm saving you just in time," Jenny noted with a smile, her jitters momentarily gone. Rafe seemed so distracted that she sort of felt sorry for him. It appealed to her feminine sense of justice to see such a tough guy looking so rattled. And so good.

"What, no comments on how beautiful your bride-to-be looks?" Miriam demanded, clearly disappointed by the verbal exchange she'd just overheard.

"You're right, Miriam. I should be horsewhipped. You look lovely, Jenny," Rafe said, taking her hand in his and kissing it.

Miriam voiced her approval. "That's more like it."

Jenny had no voice at all. Yep, that telltale heat was still there, as strong as ever. A simple touch of the hand was never simple with Rafe. It caused all kinds of stirrings deep within her.

"I've got something for you," Rafe added softly, looking into her eyes with such intensity that for a moment, Jenny could almost believe that this was a real marriage they were about to enter into. Reaching into his coat pocket, he handed her a jeweler's box.

She looked at him in confusion. "I thought we were supposed to exchange rings in the judge's chambers."

"We are. This isn't a ring. It's something else. A wedding present."

Jenny put her hand to her mouth in chagrin. "But I didn't get you anything."

"That's okay. Open it."

She did, to find a gorgeous large oval pendant suspended from a gold chain. The pendant was a sky-blue topaz so finely faceted that it glowed with a life of its own.

"It reminded me of the color of your eyes," Rafe said. "I hope you like it."

"I love it," she whispered. "Thank you."

"Here, let me put it on for you."

Turning her around, he fastened the chain. Jenny held her breath at the feel of his fingers brushing her nape. She was getting goose bumps again.

"There." He turned her so that she faced him once more. "It looks perfect on you. It falls just right." Reaching out, he used his index finger to gently move the stone against her skin. Her blouse's V neck meant that the pendant was in that sensitive zone between her collarbone and the shadowy valley of her breasts.

"Okay, you two. Enough making out on the sidewalk in public. Time to get married," Miriam announced with a grin.

Rafe offered Jenny his arm. Placing her fingers near the crook of his elbow, she took a deep breath and accompanied him inside.

The next hour was a complete blur to Jenny. She registered certain scenes, like Cindy in her flower-girl outfit, all ruffles and excitement. Rafe's dad was best man, and the beaming pride and happiness on his face gave her confidence. Miriam tearfully sniffed into her lace handkerchief. And then it was over. Jenny had said I do; so had Rafe. It was time to seal their vows with a kiss.

This part made her nervous. Her voice hadn't quivered before, but she was trembling now. Taking her shoulders in his hands, Rafe leaned down and kissed her. Once. Briefly. And then it was over almost as soon as it had begun. Jenny was being bear hugged by Chuck and Spud, then embraced by a still-tearful Miriam.

She didn't really have time to dwell on Rafe's brief kiss as they were whisked by limo to Murphy's, where a crowd of well-wishers was waiting to greet them.

One of the many well-wishers was Jenny's attorney, Miranda. Later, during a brief lull in the hubbub of activities, the two women finally got a chance to talk privately. "That was a very equitable prenup you and Rafe signed, protecting your premarital property. I am glad you took that precaution, regardless of how your marriage turns out. Oh, and I meant to tell you that I put the paperwork on your grandmother's estate through for you as you requested," Miranda said, "so you should be getting the settlement shortly."

"Great. Thanks a lot, Miranda. MegaToys won't be pleased, but I am."

"Have they given you any more trouble?"

"No, things have been quiet, although I did get a phone call the other day from the big man himself, Peter Vanorne. He called the day after I spoke with you."

"What did he say?"

"He wanted to know if I'd changed my mind about them by any chance."

"And you said?"

"That I hadn't and never would. Vanborne didn't sound very pleased, I can tell you."

"Did you tell him about your suspicions that he was behind the trouble you've been having?" Miranda asked.

"No. I didn't want to tip my hand. Besides, I don't have sufficient proof yet, and I wouldn't put it past him to turn the tables and charge me with libel or slander or whatever."

"You did the right thing."

"I sure hope so," Jenny murmured, looking at her new husband and hoping she'd done the right thing with this marriage, as well.

Two hours later, Jenny eased one foot out of her new shoes and murmured to her new husband seated beside her, "Do you remember having said something about a *small* reception?"

Rafe nodded ruefully. "To Pop, this *is* small. Once he got hold of the guest list, there was no turning back."

She wondered if Rafe had wanted to turn back. "Do you mind?"

"No. Why should I?"

Because he'd been married before, to a woman he'd truly loved, while this was merely a marriage of convenience for them both. Jenny tried hard to dismiss the kernels of uncertainty. She was helped by the distraction of cutting the five-tiered marzipan cake Hugo had created for them.

Rafe placed his hand atop hers as they both slid the cake knife into the cake. He stood so close behind her that she could feel him breathing. She felt as if she belonged in the circle of his arms. It was a dangerous feeling and one that made her nervous. Because she couldn't afford to belong to Rafe. This was just a temporary arrangement between them.

She skittered away from him the second the cake was cut.

"Wait a second. You've got to feed it to each other now. With your fingers. It's good luck," Miriam said.

Oh-oh. Jenny knew she was getting in deeper waters here. But she was a woman with moxie, she reminded herself. She could handle this—no problem. So she took a piece of the cake while Rafe held the plate. She did fine until she held it to his mouth and his lips brushed her fingertips. Then she almost dumped the cake down his pristine white shirtfront!

Luckily he moved in time to save the day. He fed her with no mishaps. But then he had more experience with this marriage stuff, she thought crossly.

The first dance was next. Miriam had hired a fleet of Viennese violinists to provide the music, and they were now in full force, creating a stirring rendition of a Strauss Waltz.

Jenny barely had time to swallow her cake before Rafe swept her into his arms and whirled her off in a waltz.

It was the first time they'd ever danced together, she realized with shock. She'd married a man she'd never even danced with. But then this was no ordinary marriage. And Rafe was no ordinary man, she thought to herself, remembering the telltale sensual warmth that had stolen through her the instant she'd placed her hand in his.

When he'd placed his arm around her waist and swirled her onto the small dance floor, the sensual warmth had been turned up another few degrees. And when he tugged her closer, she felt as if she'd stepped right into a blast furnace.

He was a good dancer—very smooth. But then she should have expected that a man who moved with his catlike stealth would be a great dancer. Waltzing with him was like gliding on a cloud. It was even better than eating chocolate frosting straight from the can!

Jenny followed his lead, instinctively responding to his every move. She was giddy with delight and couldn't hide the fact. She was sure her smile showed how she felt. For a moment in time she wasn't Jenny Benjamin-Murphy whose father had left and whose husband had only married her to save his daughter. She was just a woman in the arms of a handsome man who made her feel as if she were Cinderella at the ball.

But like Cinderella, when the clock struck twelve, the fantasy would stop and she'd have to be prepared to return to her old life—alone.

"*Oy!* What a party!" Miriam exclaimed, as Rafe deposited a breathless Jenny at her side.

"It's been a great party," Rafe agreed. "But it's about time for us to leave."

"Jenny has to toss the bouquet, don't forget," Miriam said.

Jenny did toss the bouquet, but with a little too much force. She turned around just in time to see it sail right over the crowd of expectant single women, barely miss Hugo—who looked horrified—only to be caught by Cindy.

Amid the resultant laughter, Rafe beamed in proud pleasure of the catch his daughter had made. "My daughter, the shortstop," Rafe noted.

"Your daughter, the next one to get married," Rafe's dad inserted with a grin.

Jenny watched in amusement as Rafe's proud papa smile turned to a scowl with a hint of dismay at things yet to come in his road of fatherhood. "No way. She's not even going to be allowed to date until after she's thirty!"

There wasn't time for more conversation as Rafe attempted to make a quick getaway before his dad had a chance to prepare too much of a send-off, but it was already too late. Holding hands so they wouldn't get separated in the jostling crowd, Rafe and Jenny ran out of Murphy's in a positive downpour of tossed rice, supplied to all the guests by a beaming Spud.

Jenny heard the tiny pings as the rice landed on the metal hood and roof of the Jeep. And then she heard a terrible rattle as they started to slowly drive off. Tin cans. A grinning Chuck and Spud had attached a long tail of tin cans to the Jeep's back bumper.

And so the traditions of a real wedding were complete, which left Jenny worrying about how real their honeymoon would turn out to be.

Chapter Six

"**Y**ou do understand why we had to book *one* room at this inn we're going to, right?" Rafe said. He'd just gotten back into the Jeep after pulling over to the side of the road to take off the noisy pile of cans.

"I understand," Jenny replied. "Your former mother-in-law might check up on us, and as you said, we do have to keep up appearances for Cindy's sake."

"That's right. Althea has already been snooping around. I heard that she actually had the nerve to phone some of the guests who were invited to the reception and give them the third degree."

"That's not all she had the nerve to do," Jenny muttered.

"What do you mean?" Rafe demanded.

"Forget it."

"No way. She didn't... Don't tell me she called you?"

Jenny nodded. "I wasn't going to say anything."

Rafe swore under his breath. "Getting on my case is one thing," he muttered. "But badgering you is something I won't stand for. What did she say to you?"

"Nothing I couldn't handle," Jenny replied. The woman had said that Rafe loved Susan and that no one could take her daughter's place in his life. This was nothing Jenny didn't already know, although hearing someone else say it did sting. Actually, it had hurt, but she'd gotten over it. Or so she told herself. "Besides, you'll like this tidbit of information I picked up. The woman collects artist bears."

"You're kidding me."

"I'm serious."

"How did you find that out?"

"She told me. Right before she canceled an order she'd placed with Benjamin Bear and Company a few weeks ago."

Rafe swore again. He knew how vindictive Althea could get. "I'm sorry."

"Don't be. I wouldn't want any of my bears going to her anyway. She wouldn't have given them a good home."

Rafe had to laugh at Jenny's comment. "You talk about those bears of yours as if they're real."

"They are real to me. They're my babies, my creations."

Rafe caught himself wondering if Jenny wanted to have babies of her own and then stopped himself cold. That wasn't what this marriage was all about, he reminded himself.

"My bears do take on a life of their own," Jenny was saying. "By the time I've finished putting them together and I'm doing their faces, it's as if they've come to life—each with a personality of their own. That's one of the reasons why I've expanded and hired help, so I'd have more time to create new bears while still being able to satisfy the demands for my most popular designs."

Rafe's mind was sidetracked by the idea of satisfying other demands—the kind stalking his body and making his mouth go dry.

Jenny added, "The idea of only making a design once and never again made it too difficult for me to part with the bears."

Difficult? Rafe shifted in his seat. She didn't know the meaning of the word. A flash of oncoming headlights illuminated her face as he glanced over at her. She looked so earnest sitting beside him in her white wedding suit. She clearly didn't have a clue of the lascivious nature of his thoughts. She trusted him. For now.

"So this way I have the best of both worlds—continuing the favorite designs and still creating new artist bears," Jenny concluded.

Knowing he had to contribute something or risk having her get suspicious, Rafe said, "Why do you call them artist bears? You don't mean you dress them up to look like artists, do you?"

"No. Artist bears are the ones I've done all myself—from cutting the material to making their clothing. The other bears, the ones I have help with, are artist-*designed* bears. Once the company is up and going, we should be able to ship forty or fifty of my designed bears a week, while it takes me a week to make just one bear myself."

"Seems like a lot of work for a teddy bear."

Even though it was dark inside the Jeep, he could just imagine her eyes flashing fire at him as she loftily informed him, "Some things are *worth* a lot of work."

Rafe couldn't argue with that. He also didn't know what to say to it, either. So he changed the subject. "I think everyone bought our excuse about our not being able to go on a real honeymoon because of your business opening in a few days."

"It wasn't just an excuse, it was the truth," Jenny replied. "There's no way I could leave at this point for any longer than an overnight trip."

"We couldn't avoid going away altogether," Rafe retorted. "It would have been too strange for us to just leave the reception and go upstairs together."

Jenny felt a deep twinge of pain at his comment. So he thought being with her was *strange*, did he? Just what every new wife wanted to hear, she thought bitterly. Rafe had as good as admitted that it was going to be difficult for him to get used to the idea of her living with him.

Well, no more difficult than *she'd* find it, Jenny told herself, trying to insulate herself against getting hurt any further. To do that, she focused on the one thing that was hers—her company.

"I'm amazed and very pleased with how quickly Mr. Fadden completed the renovation work on the barn," Jenny stated. "We're back on track and finally all set for the grand opening in two days."

Rafe nodded. "Fadden does good work. I could have told you that if you'd asked," he added with a patronizing assurance that really aggravated her.

How typically male of Rafe, Jenny thought in irritation, fighting the sudden urge to kick him. He'd hardly said a dozen words since they'd left Murphy's, and those he *had* said were all wrong. "Don't use that condescending tone of voice with me," she said.

"What condescending tone of voice? I was just telling you the truth."

"And telling it to me as if I didn't have two brains to rub together!"

"You're getting sensitive again," he informed her.

"And you're getting overbearing," she shot back.

There was silence after that. Jenny sat on her side of the Jeep, staring out the side window, wondering how many couples had started off on their honeymoon with an argument.

While reflecting on that thought, Jenny restlessly twisted the gold band on her finger. She wasn't used to wearing rings anymore. They got in her way, catching on material she was trying to sew. This ring was wide and smooth, with a row of diamonds channel set so that it served as both engagement and wedding ring. The gold was warm against her skin in a way strangely reminiscent of Rafe's touch. She sighed.

Hearing that sigh, Rafe would have given a night's take at Murphy's to know what Jenny was thinking. She was acting as skittish as a cat: quick to react, never at ease, waiting for trouble. It looked as though it was going to be a long night.

Once they reached the inn, and were shown to their room, things got even more awkward. Jenny noticed that Rafe couldn't wait to dump their luggage and leave the room to return downstairs to the inn's three-star restaurant. She wondered if he viewed this trip as a busman's holiday, a way of checking out the competition's food.

Dinner was awkward and tense. Conversation was stilted and it was all on her side. In desperation she said, "Nice weather we're having."

Nothing. No reply.

She tried again. "Warm for this late in October, isn't it?"

Still no comment from Rafe.

She tried a third time. "The leaves are really gorgeous. Are they always this colorful?"

"I guess so."

So much for Rafe's contribution to the dinner conversation. Jenny tried staying silent for a while, but that was even harder than holding a discussion, stilted though it might be.

They both spoke at once.

"Are you...?"

"Have you...?"

"You go first," Jenny said.

"No. Ladies first."

She'd forgotten what she was going to say, so she improvised. "I was just going to ask you if you were enjoying your steak."

"It's the same steak you've got."

"Mine's very good. You know, a friend of mine once told me that eating a spoonful of lime sherbet in between bites of steak arouses your taste buds and makes each bite of steak taste even better." As Jenny was talking, she kept thinking how silly she sounded. She hadn't felt this self-conscious since her high school speech class when she'd had to give a presentation on beekeeping.

Although Rafe was pretending a polite interest in what she was saying, she didn't believe he really heard a single word. She was willing to bet that he was about as interested in her comments as bees were in swimming.

It was almost a relief to escape the tension in the restaurant. Or so Jenny thought until they were in their room together. She did her best to stay out of Rafe's way as she partially unpacked her overnight bag. Actually, she kept most of her things inside, as if preparing a quick getaway should she need to make one. When she and her mother had first moved to her grandparent's house, Jenny hadn't unpacked her small bag for two weeks—keeping it stashed under her bed. The space inside of that suitcase had been *hers*. The house, the room, the bed weren't—and they might disappear as suddenly and unexpectedly as her father had.

"Why don't you use the bathroom first," Rafe suggested from his side of the room.

"Okay." Clutching her robe and pajamas, Jenny hustled into the bathroom and quickly shut the door.

The sound of her locking the door echoed over and over again in Rafe's mind. His mood darkened. She'd made it pretty clear that she still didn't trust him, despite the fact that he'd been on his best behavior all during their engagement. Their *short* engagement, he reminded himself. A whole ten days' worth, during which time he'd had to spend more time than usual at work with bookings for two private parties, a bar mitzvah and a wedding reception in addition to his own.

Jenny had been getting progressively more on edge since their reception. She'd looked tense all through dinner, and as fragile as glass. She was probably afraid he was going to jump her and ravish her in one fell swoop.

Rafe was determined to prove her wrong. He was going to be a perfect gentleman tonight if it killed him, and it just might, the way he was feeling right now.

All through dinner he hadn't been able to concentrate. Instead, his attention had been fixed on Jenny's mouth as she'd licked whipped cream from her upper lip after daintily having taken a bite of chocolate cream pie. It wasn't that he hadn't been listening to her, he had. But he kept getting distracted by that sexy combination of fire and ice in her voice—a voice that had a hold on him and wouldn't let go.

Rafe yet again reminded himself that he'd given Jenny his word that he wouldn't push her into anything. There was time left. They'd have the next five years. His eyes wandered toward the bed. They didn't have to fall onto the king-size bed and make love tonight—slow, hot sex that didn't stop until they were both too satiated to move a single muscle. Kisses that started at fingertips and progressed all the way down the body—he kissing her, she kissing him. Clothes discarded. Bodies slickly joined. Pulsing, throbbing....

Swearing under his breath, Rafe straightened and turned away from the bed. Striding over to the window, he yanked it open and inhaled lungfuls of crisp autumn air.

"Are you all right?" Jenny tentatively asked from the threshold of the bathroom.

"Fine," Rafe grated. "I just need to get some fresh air. I'll be back in a few minutes."

He was gone before she could say a word. Great, she thought to herself. He was probably thinking about his wife, his *real* wife—the one he'd loved—and that explained the pained expression on his face.

It was becoming pretty clear to her that Rafe couldn't even stand to be in the same room with her, Jenny noted, her lips starting to tremble, a sure sign that tears were imminent. Not the most auspicious way to start a marriage.

She smoothed back the covers on the bed, trying to keep herself busy and keep the tears at bay. She supposed she and Rafe should have discussed the sleeping arrangements earlier. Not that she was really worried; Rafe had assured her that he had only married her for his daughter's sake. Jenny realized she was a useful means to an end, that's all.

And while she anticipated that at some point their relationship might well turn intimate, she hadn't expected it to happen overnight. Most people who got married loved each other...or lusted after each other enough to mistake it for love, she amended cynically.

Such was not the case with her and Rafe. They each had practical reasons, good reasons for their decision to get married. Neither love nor lust had played a part.

Okay, maybe a little lust on her part, she allowed. And Rafe found her attractive enough. Sometimes. When he wasn't thinking about his perfect Susan.

The door opened and he was back. She tightened her robe around her waist. The air was thick enough to cut it with a knife.

"You go ahead...." Rafe said, indicating the bed with one hand. "I'm just going to watch a little TV before turning in."

Having said that, he reached for the remote control, sat down in the armchair near the sitting area of the large room and was seemingly totally engrossed in a nighttime football game within seconds. He didn't move a muscle as she removed her robe and slid into bed.

"Okay if I turn out the light by the bed?" she asked, her throat feeling twisted and parched.

"Fine with me," he said.

She lay there for almost an hour. She really thought she'd mastered the urge to cry that had been hounding her since they'd arrived. She was wrong. The tears came quietly, but all at once—although Rafe was still so immersed in the game that she doubted he even noticed.

Again she was wrong. "What's the matter?" Rafe asked from beside the bed.

"Nothing." She kept her face partially buried under the sheet and tried not to sniff.

"Can't you sleep?"

"I'll be all right in a minute."

"Okay," Rafe said.

She couldn't believe it. The idiot was taking her word for it and going back to his stupid game!

She sat up, suddenly furious. "Look, it's not every day that I get married! It's no surprise than I'm sitting here crying like an idiot. And I never cry!" She sniffed. "Never! I hate crying. Especially in front of strangers."

"I'm not exactly a stranger," Rafe dryly pointed out. "I'm your husband now."

"Well, I'm not used to crying in front of husbands, either," she said on a gulp as her crying jag really started in earnest.

"It's okay," he said soothingly, returning to the bed to sit beside her and tug her close until she rested against his chest.

"I'll get your shirt all wet," she mumbled.

"That's okay. I'll survive."

"It's stress. And exhaustion," Jenny tried explaining, although the tears and occasional hiccups were at odds with her rational tone of voice. "I haven't been getting much sleep for the past few days."

"I know." He leaned back against the pillows, carefully swinging his legs onto the mattress—moving slowly, so as not to spook her any further. "Just close your eyes and rest." He threaded his fingers through her hair, his touch soothing. "Trust me, everything will seem much better once you get some rest."

Once she was finally all cried out, Jenny's eyes felt heavy. She really was beat. Between getting ready for the wedding and for Benjamin Bear and Company's grand opening, she'd been averaging only four or five hours' sleep for the past week. She'd just close her eyes for a minute, that's all....

When Jenny finally opened her eyes again, it was light outside and she was still snuggled against Rafe. At some point during the night he'd pulled the covers up around them both. His white shirt was badly wrinkled and she suspected his slacks were equally rumpled. He didn't look very comfortable leaning back against the pillow he'd propped behind himself last night.

As if aware of her gaze on him, Rafe suddenly opened his eyes. His dark blue eyes stared into hers, searching her face before settling on her parted lips. By the time she recognized his intent, he was already bending his head to kiss her. But before his mouth brushed her, he groaned and straightened, ruefully rubbing a sudden muscle spasm cause by a crick in his neck. "I'm getting too old for this," he muttered.

Jenny felt responsible for his current predicament. "I'm sorry about crying all over your shoulder last night. You didn't have to hold me all night."

Rafe shrugged. "You were feeling lonely—"

"Lonely?" She jerked away from him as if she'd been stuck with a cattle prod. "You thought I was lonely so you felt sorry for me and that's why you were nice to me?"

"That's not what I said."

"But it's what you meant."

"Don't go telling me what I meant. I know what I meant."

"Then tell me."

Rafe muttered darkly under his breath. "This is ridiculous."

"I agree. I can assure you that there's no need for you to feel sorry for me."

"I wasn't feeling sorry for you," he growled.

"Then what were you feeling?"

"This." He tugged her into his arms. Holding her the way he was, she could feel his arousal. "Does that feel like pity?"

She wasn't going to give in that easily this time. "You can't yank me into your arms every time you want to prove a point to me," she retorted.

"I give up." He was practically seething with male exasperation.

"And don't you dare try to kiss me until we've got this settled," she warned him, recognizing that look in his eyes.

"Why not?" He nuzzled his way from her neck to her temple. "This seems to be the way we communicate the best."

"I can't think when you do that."

"So don't think."

"You said you wouldn't push me," she reminded him.

Rafe reluctantly pulled away to frown at her. "That doesn't mean that you can melt in my arms and not expect me to respond."

"Oh, so now this is all *my* fault?" She jumped out of bed to stare down at him, her hands propped on her hips in anger. "You really take the cake, you know that, Murphy?"

"You're a Murphy now, too. And don't you forget it," he said.

"I don't have time to stand around arguing with you."

"Isn't this where I walked in?" Rafe noted mockingly, remembering their first argument the first time they'd met. She'd had her hands on her hips then, too. Drawing his attention to their soft curves then as she was now.

"This is why I want to wait before we go any further," Jenny was telling him. "Because the only time we aren't arguing is when we're . . ." Her voice trailed off. Something about the heated hunger of his gaze made her drop her hands to her sides, before defensively wrapping them around her middle, as if to shield herself from his view. "What I mean is that we have to learn to get along better."

"A little hard to do when you keep misinterpreting everything I say and do," Rafe retorted, irritated by the way she'd gone from avenging angel to schoolmarm.

His anger provoked her own. "Maybe if you told me what you were thinking every once in a while I wouldn't feel in the dark where you're concerned," Jenny shot back. "Your precious Susan may have been able to read your mind, but I can't."

Jenny knew she'd made a mistake even as she saw Rafe's expression harden before closing up tighter than a drum.

She tried to make amends. "We just need some more time to get to know each other better—"

He cut her off. "Fine. Take your time." Stalking into the bathroom, he slammed the door. Seconds later she heard the shower running.

She felt like running herself—right out the nearest exit! She'd really stirred things up now by committing the major sin of referring to Susan. But until Rafe worked things out, Jenny wasn't about to fall into bed with him as a handy way for him to forget his precious wife for a few hours.

She knew she hadn't wanted his love, and she told herself she still didn't. But when he made love to her, she didn't want the ghost of his dead wife in bed with them, either. Surely that wasn't too much to ask?

Breakfast that morning was just as tense as dinner had been last night. Jenny felt as if her stomach were in knots.

"Would you just relax?" Rafe growled. "I'm not going to leap over the table and ravish you, so you can calm down and release your death grip on that fork."

"Look, this isn't going to work if we're at each other's throats every minute." Jenny blushed, recalling the way he'd nibbled her throat a short time ago. "What I mean is, we should try and get along. I know it's awkward learning to live with someone."

"How do you know that?" he asked suspiciously, the thought of her living with another man making his blood boil.

"It was awkward when we moved in with my grandparents when I was a kid," Jenny replied. "But it worked out in the end. All I'm saying is that maybe we should call a truce during this period of adjustment."

"A truce?"

"Yes. You know, a temporary cease-fire."

"With each of us returning to our respective corners, is that it?"

She nodded.

"Fine." He shrugged. "If that's the way you want it."

Jenny didn't know what she wanted anymore, and that shook her, but no more so than the idea of sharing a bedroom with Rafe for the next five years. Because once they returned to his place, that's exactly what they'd be doing.

Chapter Seven

"Daddy, you're back! I missed you!" Cindy exclaimed as she ran out to meet them the second they pulled up in front of Murphy's.

Leaning down, Rafe swung his daughter up into his arms. "I missed you, too, pumpkin."

"I got a question, Daddy."

"You've usually got a million of 'em, kiddo. Go ahead, shoot. What do you want to know this time?" he asked, praying it wasn't where babies came from again.

"Should I call Jenny Mommy now?" Cindy asked him.

Rafe knew he should have been prepared for this, and mentally he was. But there was no pretending he didn't feel a twinge of guilt at Susan's memory. To his surprise, Jenny came to his rescue.

"You can still call me Jenny, if you'd like to," she told Cindy. "I won't mind. And if you do feel comfortable calling me Mommy someday that would be fine, too. I'd be your second mommy."

"That sounds okay. You know what?" Cindy held out her hand to show her where the polish had been chipped even though Jenny had just done Cindy's nails a few days before. "My nails went funny."

Jenny's heart had just gone "funny" at the ease with which Cindy had accepted her. At least one member of the Murphy family didn't think it was strange having her around.

"Hey, kiddo, give Jenny a few hours to get settled in first before trying to wheedle her into painting those fancy nails of yours, okay?" Rafe inserted, setting his daughter back on her feet.

"Was your moneymoon impressive?" Cindy asked.

"It's *honey*moon and it was fine," Rafe said.

"What can I carry, Daddy? I want to carry something, too," Cindy insisted as Rafe unpacked the Jeep. "Did you bring your pillow? Everyone knows you have to bring a pillow if you're going for a sleep over."

"I can see why," Rafe noted, shooting Jenny a meaningful look while absently rubbing his neck which still wasn't back to normal yet.

Grabbing her overnight bag, Jenny headed inside. Murphy's wasn't open for business yet, so she walked through the empty restaurant toward the stairway that led to their private quarters. As she made her way upstairs, she realized she was doing so for the first time as Rafe's wife.

She'd been in Rafe's bedroom before, when she'd moved several boxes of her things over from her house. She knew that the entire third floor, formerly an attic, had been transformed into a master bedroom suite, complete with skylights and a private bathroom. There wasn't much furniture—a chest of drawers and the matching huge king-size four-poster bed, which Rafe confessed he'd simply ordered out of a catalog. There were two walk-in closets, so she'd stored her things in one of those.

Jenny paused, awkwardly standing near the bedroom's threshold as if afraid to venture farther inside. She felt the presence of his first wife very strongly at that moment.

As if able to read her mind, from behind her Rafe softly said, "Susan never slept up here. The third floor renovations weren't completed until after her death. We shared the extra bedroom downstairs and I got this furniture when I moved up here. We'll need another chest of drawers for you," he said matter-of-factly.

To Jenny's eyes, the room looked open and empty. The plush carpeting was dark blue and the white walls were bare—not a painting or poster in sight.

"This is your home now, so feel free to make any changes up here you think necessary," Rafe added.

It didn't feel like home to her. She'd barely had time to settle into her place, and here she was moving next door. Jenny didn't know what she was going to do with her house, she hadn't planned that part through yet. But she was hanging on to it for now—just in case.

"We should probably discuss the sleeping arrangements," Rafe continued. "We'll be sharing this room for the same reason we shared the one last night."

Jenny nodded her understanding.

"I've got an old army cot I picked up at a surplus store that I can set up here until things get settled."

"That would be fine for me," Jenny quickly agreed.

"It wasn't meant for you. I meant I'd sleep on it."

"Nonsense." He already held her responsible for ruining his neck, Jenny wasn't about to put him out any further. "I'll sleep on it."

"It's not very comfortable," he warned her.

"That's okay."

"Fine. Have it your way. Although, I should point out that the bed is large enough to safely sleep the two of us without any problem."

Problem? Is that what he considered her to be? She stiffened with resentment. "The cot will be fine."

"Suit yourself."

Of course, the cot *wasn't* fine, Jenny discovered as she tried to sleep on it that night. For one thing, it was too narrow for her to even turn around in. For another, the thing was a killer for lower back pain. She sighed, longing for a can of chocolate frosting to make her feel better. But she didn't want Rafe catching her overdosing on frosting, so she'd left all her cans at home in her kitchen. She'd also left her wonderfully soft sheets at home, on her incredibly soft mattress. . . .

She sighed again.

"This is ridiculous," Rafe growled. Sitting up in bed, he switched on the light. "You're not going to get any sleep on that thing." Leaning over, he threw back the covers on the other side of the huge bed. "Come on, get over here."

Jenny hesitated.

"Look, you've got nothing to fear from me tonight," he assured her, before adding the challenge, "unless it's yourself you don't trust?"

She eyed him suspiciously. "How do I know you won't try any funny stuff?"

"Because I'm not in a humorous mood," Rafe replied with a glare. "Now, are you going to come and sleep here or are you going to stay on that bed of nails?"

Head bent, Jenny decided that injured pride was better than a permanently injured spine. Wearing yet another pair of pajamas, she scooted over to the bed and got under the covers—lying there hugging the very edge of the mattress.

This time it was Rafe who sighed. "You go to sleep that way and you'll probably end up falling out of bed and breaking your leg," he told her. "Reach out behind you, there's about a mile of open mattress there just waiting for you to get comfortable in."

Jenny did as he suggested, and sure enough there seemed to be plenty of space. She ruefully acknowledged that she must look like an idiot, clinging to the edge of the bed like a rock climber suddenly struck with vertigo. Relaxing, she made herself comfortable. Her last thought before drifting off to sleep was a mental note to buy new sheets for this bed, nice smooth sheets like the ones she had at home.

Rafe stared down at her, amazed at the quickness with which she'd fallen asleep. The pale moonlight streaming down through the skylights provided enough illumination for him to see her profile—the curve of her high cheekbone, the alabaster paleness of her ear, the lush length of her lashes.

Seeing the loose strand of hair falling over her face, Rafe automatically reached out to smooth it away. Her creamy skin was soft and so touchable. There, in the darkness, Rafe admitted that he was feeling more than he wanted to for his new wife. And frankly, that panicked him. Last night she'd said they needed more time. Now he was prone to agree with her. He needed more time to fight this attraction that was threatening to become more than just attraction. So he was putting the brakes on his desire—before things got out of control and he ended up crashing.

Jenny woke up feeling sheltered and protected. It took her a second or two to realize that she'd woken in Rafe's arms for the second morning in a row. She was starting to make a habit of this and she wasn't sure that was a wise thing to do.

Even so, it felt too good for her to move just yet. He was still asleep, thank goodness. So she just stayed where she was, her cheek and her hand resting against his chest—his bare chest. The warm and spicy scent of his skin tickled her nose. Her hand rose and fell with every breath he took. If she listened carefully, she could even hear his heart beating. *Kaa-boom. Kaa-boom.* She smiled.

She enjoying being in his arms, liked listening to the even tenor of his breathing. I could get used to this, Jenny thought with a grin. And that's the problem. Her grin faded as her misgivings returned. It wouldn't do for her to depend on Rafe too much. Their situation was temporary and their emotions... totally messed up, Jenny admitted with a sigh. At least hers for Rafe were.

She was attracted to him. Very much so. Irresistibly so. And that wasn't all. He also inspired lust, admiration, affection, irritation, anger, lust—the list went on and on.

And what about love? a little voice in her head whispered. Wouldn't you like to have it all? To have him love you the way he'd loved Susan? To have him look at you as if the sun rose and set with you, as if you were the center of his universe?

No good wishing for what you can't have, her grandfather had sternly warned her when, as a child, she'd cried herself to sleep wishing for a kitten. It's just a waste of time.

What would a woman with moxie do in a situation like this? Jenny wondered to herself. Go after what she wanted, she answered herself.

Propping herself up on one elbow, Jenny looked down at Rafe's sleeping face. He looked good. Tired, but very, very good. She was tempted to trace the curve of his lips, but settled for brushing the rumpled thickness of his dark hair off his forehead. He turned toward her, as if seeking more of her touch. And then he whispered a name. "Susan..."

Jenny leapt from the bed as if scalded, not caring that she woke Rafe in the process.

"Wha-at?" Rafe's eyes flew open in time to see Jenny stalking toward the bathroom, where she slammed the door shut.

Sitting up in bed, he frowned, still disoriented from the dream he'd just had about Susan. He'd been trying to follow her, but when he was just about to reach her, she'd turned, shaking her head and gesturing that he go back. Go back to what? Rafe wondered. To Jenny?

Jenny stood in the shower, letting the hot water wash some sense into her. What did it take for her to get the message? she asked herself while scrubbing herself with the loofa she'd brought from home. It's no use wishing for what you can't have. Just a waste of time. And chances were that when you got it, it wouldn't last anyway, she added.

It wasn't until she was toweling herself dry with her ultrasoft Egyptian cotton bath sheet that she realized she'd left all her clothes in the bedroom, having forgotten to grab something to wear when she'd dashed out of bed. Which left her with little choice but to wrap the bath sheet around herself. She didn't have time to waste here. She had things to do—a grand opening to take care of. Today was the big day and she wasn't going to let anything ruin it. Or anyone. Rafe included.

Straightening her shoulders, she stalked out of the bathroom and headed directly for her closet without looking once at Rafe, who was still lounging in bed.

"You know, I always wondered how women do that," he murmured. "How *do* you keep an entire towel up with that little knot thing at the top? I've tried it, but I put a towel around me, take one step and it's in a pile at my feet."

Imagining the picture Rafe would make standing with a towel at his feet, wearing nothing but drops of water from the shower, momentarily distracted Jenny from the search for her intended outfit for the day. But only momentarily. She resolutely dismissed the erotic picture from her mind and reached for her sage-green silk pant suit. Grabbing underwear, her bra and a white top, she returned to the bathroom, without deigning to answer Rafe's rhetorical question.

"Why do I get the feeling you're mad at me?" Jenny heard Rafe inquire through the thickness of the wooden bathroom door.

"Probably because I *am* mad at you," she replied.

"Care to tell me why?"

"No."

"I'm supposed to read your mind, is that it?" he said as she opened the door.

Giving him a dismissive look, she merely said, "Have a nice day, Rafe. I'm outta here."

"Wait a second. Where are you going?"

"To work. My grand opening is today in case you forgot."

"I didn't forget." Several days ago, he'd offered to accompany her to the opening, but she'd quickly told him that she'd be nervous enough without him being there. So he'd arranged to have some flowers sent over instead.

Watching her, Rafe silently noted that Jenny looked great in the soft green pant suit. The silky material lovingly draped her body, tempting him to reach out and see if she felt as good as she looked. Closing his eyes, Rafe could still see the creamy curve of her breasts and a shadow valley of her cleavage....

Stung by the way he'd closed his eyes and consequently his thoughts from her, Jenny said, "No, you don't forget things do you? You hang on to the past and you don't let go."

He gave her a look of male aggravation. "I could say the same about you."

"Meaning what?"

"Meaning I'm not the only one with scars, Jenny."

"No, but you're the only one who says another person's name when we're in bed together!" Having said that, she left.

* * *

"You're early," Miriam complained when Jenny walked into the barn. "I'm not ready here for you yet. Go back outside."

"What are you doing up on that ladder?"

"Painting my nails," Miriam retorted. "What does it look like I'm doing? I'm trying to put up a sign. A banner, really. And it's not cooperating. Neither are you. This was supposed to be a surprise."

"I can't get into my office, Miriam."

"That's right. You're not supposed to get in there. Not until we do the ribbon-cutting ceremony."

"What ribbon-cutting ceremony?"

"The one to open our new facility here. What, you thought we should use a magnum of champagne against the side of the doorway instead? That's for ships, not buildings."

"Where did all these flowers come from?" Jenny asked.

"The florist," Miriam mumbled around a mouthful of nails. "Enough with the questions, already. Stand here and be useful."

"Yes, ma'am," Jenny teasingly replied.

"Ma'am-schma'am," Miriam retorted. "You've ruined my surprise. You should look suitably remorseful."

Jenny rearranged her grin into a sorrowful look. "Is that better?"

"Much. Hand me the hammer, would you?"

"Let me do that," Jenny insisted.

Miriam didn't need telling twice. Once their positions were reversed, Jenny hammered the small nails into place for yet another banner.

Noticing the way Jenny wielded the hammer with vehement flourish, Miriam said, "So how was the honeymoon?"

"Fine." Jenny hit the nail even harder.

"You and Rafe didn't have a fight by any chance, did you?"

"What makes you ask that?"

"The fact that you're hammering hard enough to drive that nail all the way to China."

"Men are impossible," Jenny stated.

"Are you referring to the gender in general or one in particular?"

Jenny sighed. "Don't mind me. I just want everything to go right today."

"It will," Miriam said confidently. "We'll have the big celebration...."

"So long as it's not so big that we have to invite the governor," Jenny mockingly inserted.

"You sure? I've got connections," Miriam said. "I could have gotten the governor here."

"I'm sure. Unlike the wedding, I'd like this to be small scale."

"You didn't like your wedding?" Miriam looked hurt.

"I didn't mean that exactly."

"Then what exactly?"

"I'm nervous," Jenny admitted.

"Of what?"

"Failing."

"That won't happen. You're no *schlemazel.*"

"Is that good or bad?" Jenny asked.

"Let me put it this way—there's an old folk saying that when a *schlemazel* winds a clock, it stops. And when he sells umbrellas, the sun comes out."

"So you're saying I'm not a loser?"

"Bingo! So enough already with all these worries. You're already a success in my book, and that's the only one that counts." Miriam grinned.

Jenny hugged her. "What did I ever do to deserve a friend like you?"

"Must have been something really good," the irrepressible Miriam replied.

"Must have been," Jenny agreed with a smile.

"I've got a special hat for this occasion." Miriam put it on to model it for Jenny. "See? It's purple and it's got teddy bears appliquéd to the side. I added the Benjamin Bear logo myself and embroidered it on. Pretty nifty, huh?"

"It's great. What did Max say about it?"

"That it was a work of art. After thirty years of marriage, he's finally learning."

"That's because you're such a good teacher, Miriam," Jenny stated with a grin.

"That's one of the many reasons why I like you," the older woman replied. "Because you have such good taste. Who'd have thought when we met at that teddy-bear show five years ago that we'd end up here like this?"

"Do you remember the lady who cried when she came back near the end of the show to find someone else buying the bear she wanted?"

Miriam nodded. "I remember. Or how about that guy who bought Bertram Bear because he looked just like his uncle?"

"And then there was the devoted bear collector that carried Benjamin Bear around the entire show in his backpack, with Benjamin's arm raised as if he were waving at the crowd."

"You sure got a lot of new customers from that," Miriam noted.

"I got a letter from that collector just the other day, telling me his bear was doing just fine."

"All your bears are doing just fine. Look at them." Miriam gestured toward the large display area they'd spent most of last week setting up—not just for the opening today, but also for those occasions when buyers stopped by.

Benjamin and Bonita were sitting together on a specially made park bench like a courting couple. Nearby, a one-of-a-kind Bambino Bear, wearing a cowboy hat and boots, was sitting astride a small wooden rocking horse. Mischievous Bertram Bear sat with a pile of wooden blocks in front of him, a bright blue bow around his neck, while Grandfather Bear—comfortable in his rocking chair with his spectacles and a newspaper in his lap—looked on.

In a separate gathering were most of Jenny's one-of-a-kind originals, many of them clothed. There was Teddy, the college student complete with varsity sweater and schoolbag. Theodora, made out of fluffy white mohair, was dressed in Victorian elegance complete with lacy pantaloons and a flowered bonnet. Bernie Bear, in a sailor suit, had a wooden sailboat. She'd placed Boyo Bear in a stand so that he stood upright next to a foam snowman she'd made as part of the exhibit; and then she'd drizzled both of them with fake snow.

Jenny's own personal collection of other artists' bears that she'd bought over the years, including those of Mary Holstad, Sue Cole and Beverly Port, she kept in a special display cabinet at home. Funny how she still couldn't consider Rafe's place to be home yet. But this . . . this was all hers.

Jenny looked around her new studio, wanting every detail to be just right. She checked the holder storing spools of thread: regular poly/cotton sewing thread, Perle cotton embroidery thread for the noses and mouths and medium-weight nylon fishing line for sewing the eyes. The other tools of her trade—from the curved upholstery needles for sewing on the ears to the T-shaped stuffing tools—were all neatly placed in clear plastic bins on the worktables. Two new sewing machines also stood ready.

Spread out on one table were samples of possible new materials—tipped mohair with darker hairs woven into the pile, a swirly mohair in a lovely dusty lavender shade and an inventive synthetic fabric with an inch-long stringy pile. The material Jenny selected for each of her designs lent them all a different look and consequently different characters. She fingered the samples, wondering what kind of bear each would create.

"Stop your fussing already," Miriam teasingly told her. "Time to open up. Your public, not to mention your employees and Max with the video camera, await you outside. You did it, Jenny...." Miriam gave her a giant bear hug. "You made your dream come true."

Jenny didn't return to Rafe's house until after eight. It had been a busy day, but they'd gotten a lot done, making a large dent in the back orders that had been piling up. The local press had shown up for the opening, taking several photos of Jenny and her bears. She felt the satisfaction that came from knowing she'd done a good day's work, and seen her vision transformed into a number of completed bears with the help of her new studio workers—one woman who did cutting and stuffing, another who did hand sewing and a third who was a whiz on the sewing machine.

Jenny still did the finishing work on all the bears herself, using an electric hair clipper to shave each bear's muzzle, sewing on the nose and mouth and trimming with sharp scissors. She often spent over two hours working on each bear's face to produce just the right expression.

In fact, she'd pricked her finger again while embroidering on the nose and mouth of one of her bears. Since a metal thimble interfered with her sense of touch too much, Jenny had taken to using a leather thimble, which usually did the trick.

Looking at the tiny wound, she remembered that last time she'd pricked herself with a needle. She'd gone to Mount Washington and had that picnic with Cindy and Rafe the next day. That's when he'd taken her fingers and kissed them. It had been the first time she'd ever felt his lips on her skin. She should have known then that he'd be a major force in her life. Instead, she'd foolishly thought she had everything under control. Now she knew better.

Rafe had dinner waiting for her when she came in. He took one look at her, sat her in a chair at the table in his private dining room and placed a plate in front of her. It smelled heavenly. "What is it?"

"Thumper," he retorted.

She raised startled eyes to his. "This is rabbit?" She shook her head. "I couldn't."

"I had a feeling you'd feel that way about it. No, rabbit is the specialty tonight, but this is veal. *Tournedos de veau à l'oseille,* to be exact. Veal in fresh sorrel sauce," he translated when Jenny frowned.

"If there's any rabbit in here, I'll strangle you in your sleep," she promised him.

Jenny thought she heard Rafe mutter something about her being the death of him anyway as he walked away to deal with a crisis in the kitchen.

The dinner was delicious as was the *crème caramel* for dessert. The rich custard-and-caramel dessert slid smoothly along her tongue as she ate every last bit.

"Cindy's waiting for you to tuck her in," Rafe said as he rejoined her.

They went upstairs together where they found Chuck holding down the fort, trying unsuccessfully to interest Cindy into hearing *Moby Dick.*

"Read me *Sleeping Beauty,*" Cindy instructed Rafe and Jenny. "Only this time you've gotta kiss Jenny like it says in the book," Cindy added.

"Orders from headquarters," Chuck noted with a grin before he left the three of them alone.

As Jenny read her lines aloud, her thoughts were on that upcoming moment when the prince kissed the lovely Princess Aurora, awakening her from her slumbers. She told herself that Rafe would probably skip over that part, as he

had the last time that his daughter had suggested they act
out the part as written.

But she should have know that Rafe rarely reacted the way
she expected him to. When the moment came, he leaned toward the side of the bed where Jenny sat immobilized by the
devilish gleam she saw in his dark blue eyes. His daughter
was watching, she frantically reminded herself. There wasn't
much he could do to her . . . was there? Maybe he'd just kiss
her fingers again, like he had on their picnic.

Rafe was subtle, but he was seductive. And he kissed her
mouth, not her fingers. His lips touched hers, and while to
an innocent onlooker the kiss may have seemed princely,
from Jenny's vantage point it was downright hot.

"And they lived happily ever after," Rafe murmured,
barely lifting his lips from hers.

Cindy applauded enthusiastically before jumping up and
joining them for a three-way embrace. "I like happy endings the best!" she exclaimed.

So did Jenny, but the problem was that she hadn't really
believed in them since she was Cindy's age.

"Great news!" Rafe announced as he joined Jenny in
their bedroom later that night. "I just got a call from Althea's lawyer."

"It's late for a lawyer to be calling, isn't it?" Jenny noted
with a look at the bedside clock.

"Not when you pay them what Althea pays them," Rafe
retorted. "Anyway the lawyer said that under the circumstances, what with our recent marriage and your good reputation, he's advised Althea to drop her request for sole
custody of Cindy and to settle for guaranteed visitation
rights."

"But she's got those already, doesn't she? You've never
tried to stop her from visiting Cindy, have you?"

"No, I haven't," he said. "But Althea is paranoid. She
wants those rights guaranteed, so I agreed. I never wanted

to keep her from Cindy. I just didn't want her taking my daughter away from me.''

"And now she can't do that, right?"

"Right."

"That is great news," Jenny agreed with a smile. At least *something* good had come of their marriage of convenience. Actually, things were working out just as they'd planned—Rafe got to keep his daughter and Jenny got to keep her bear company. Now if she could just get her emotions into an equally tidy state....

"What's that lump in the middle of the bed?" Rafe asked as he sat down on the bed to remove his shoes.

"It's an old New England tradition," she replied. "A bundling board. To make sure we stay on our own sides of the bed," she added for extra measure.

"A rolled-up blanket is going to do that?"

"Yes. And it's a rolled-up featherbed, not just a skinny blanket. In the old days they used to use a piece of wood that went from the headboard to the footboard, but I thought we could make do with this for the time being."

Rafe reminded himself of how just last night he'd wanted to slow things down. But what his mind and what his body told him were two different things. As for his heart ... He was confused, and that irritated him. So did the so-called bundling board.

"Fine. If it makes you feel better. But we're not sleeping this way indefinitely," he warned her. "The time is going to come when we'll share this bed the way a man and wife should."

But Jenny had already decided that she wasn't about to do that until she was sure that it was *she* he was sharing his bed with, and not the memory of Susan.

"All's quiet here on the bear front," Jenny told her attorney over the phone a few days later. "I appreciate you expediting things for me the way you did."

"That's my job. You didn't have to send me that adorable teddy bear, but I'm glad you did," Miranda said. "Thomas Esquire is perfect."

"It's the first Barrister Bear I've ever made," Jenny said. "I thought you'd appreciate the legal accessories."

"I did. The law books and the briefcase were perfect. So were the yellow suspenders and the bow tie." Miranda chuckled. "In fact, I'd like to order some more for a few friends of mine."

"We should be able to do that, but we're still catching up on orders, so it might be awhile."

"That's okay. Think you could do it in time for Christmas?"

"That should be doable."

"This must be a busy season for you," Miranda noted.

"Fall is my busiest time, leading up to the holidays," Jenny replied. "Although actually every season has been busy, thank heavens."

"Which is why MegaToys wants their hands on your bears."

"I'm hoping that Peter Vanborne finally got the message that I'm not interested and that he can't scare me off. There haven't been any more incidents since I had the security system installed."

"What about that contractor who didn't complete the job? Was his name Gardner? Do you want me to take some kind of action on that?"

"I didn't pay him the remaining amount and I stopped payment on the check I'd given him two days before the roof leaked."

"If he gives you any problems about that, you just refer him to me," Miranda said.

"I will. Thanks again," Jenny said.

After hanging up, Jenny fooled around with several sketches of other possible Barrister Bears—which got her to thinking about Banker Bears, Doctor Bears. Her pencil flew over the paper as the pile of sketches and lists of ideas kept growing. Caught up in a storm of inspiration, Jenny wasn't aware of the passing of time.

She heard something. Branches hitting the side of the barn maybe? The wind appeared to be picking up. Glancing at her watch, she realized that it was after ten already. Time to call it a night.

The sound came again. This time, Jenny got up and looked out the window of her office. There was a full moon out tonight, enabling her to see the shadowy outline of a man. Rafe?

No, she realized with a shot of alarm. This man was much shorter than Rafe and his movements were very furtive. Hurrying back to her desk, Jenny immediately hit the silent alarm that would notify the police department.

What if the man left before the police got there? Maybe if she looked out her window again, she'd be able to get a clear look at him. She was cautiously moving around the front of her desk toward the window when she heard her name being bellowed. A second later Rafe showed up, seemingly out of nowhere.

"Did you see him?" she demanded.

"See who?"

"Great. Now look what you did. You scared him away with all your yelling!"

He grabbed her arm, as if fearing that she'd take off after the suspect herself. "What are you doing over here alone this late at night?" Rafe growled. "The door was open! How am I supposed to protect you when you pull a stunt like this?"

Jenny opened her mouth to growl right back at him, but Rafe prevented her from doing so by kissing her.

There was no preliminary buildup, no gentle prelude. Passion prevailed as Rafe hungrily took complete possession of her mouth, erotically nipping at her lips when she stubbornly tried to close them, tempting her until she gave in and parted them once more. Now he was free to taste the inner curve of her upper lip with the tip of his tongue.

Rafe felt her shudder in his arms. She was all fire and no more ice, fulfilling the promise in her sexy voice. She wasn't afraid of his passion. In fact, she seemed to welcome it—greeting his tongue with hers, clinging to him instead of pushing him away.

She wore a scarf around her neck. It got in his way. After fumbling a moment with the knot, he undid it and slid it off.

The sensation of her silk scarf sliding across her skin made Jenny shiver. Once he replaced the silk with the softness of his lips, she moaned in pleasure. As gentle as a summer's breeze, he brushed his mouth over her skin. With a swirl of his tongue, he delicately saluted the softness of her bare flesh as he pushed aside the collar of her shirt for further exploration.

Jenny felt as if her every nerve ending were alive and humming, making her responsive to the slightest sensation. She was highly aware of the warmth of his hands as he slid them beneath her shirt, now loosened from the waistband of her pleated skirt. The slightly rough surface of his fingertips glided over her flesh with a delicate abrasiveness, leaving a trail of pleasure everywhere he touched her.

And still he kissed her, one kiss blending into the next, as if hoping to absorb her very essence and merge it with his own. She was inundated with sensual perceptions. There were so many textures to savor—the silky hot slide of his tongue, the hard resilience of his body pressed so tightly against her own, the velvety shadow of his unshaven face that made her fingertips sing. Needing to get even closer, she looped her arms around his neck and then slid her hands through his hair, marveling at the springy thickness of it.

Jenny was only vaguely aware of him lowering her to the couch opposite her desk. All coherent thought had long since ceased and she was running on pure passion here. Which is why she was more concerned with and distracted by the fit of his body as he lowered himself on top of her than the propriety or wisdom of what they were doing.

He'd positioned his knee between her legs, increasing the shameless intimacy of their embrace. She could feel every inch of his muscular frame as he responded to the yielding softness of hers.

Breathless with excitement, she hastily began unbuttoning his shirt. It only took him a second to remove her deep V-neck sweater, tugging it over her hair in one smooth motion. She barely had a chance to grab a lungful of air before he was kissing her again, just as she wanted him to—the thrust of his tongue mirroring the surge of his hips. All the while he was undoing the remaining few buttons on her shirt and parting the white cotton, baring her to his view.

Jenny was aching with the fiery need to feel his hand upon her. She closed her eyes and sighed with pleasure as he caressed her breasts through her sheer silk bra, cupping her in the palm of his hand as he brushed the rosy crest with his thumb. The erotic friction made her gasp. Leaning down, he kissed her parted lips, tasting her next gasp as he gently worked her nipple between his thumb and index finger, rolling the firm peak with devilish skill.

Jenny had never felt this way before. Shivers of radiant pleasure were dancing down her spine even as the feminine heat of an ageless desire intensified deep within her. But this was more than just physical attraction. This was the key to her heart, the path to her very soul. This was love.

Jenny, however, had no time to reflect on this startling self-discovery before she was once again thrown into a maelstrom of sensual elation created by the wicked adoration of his mouth. Finally ending their lengthy and elaborate kiss, Rafe nibbled his way down her throat and across her collarbone. Expectation curled its way through her as he neared the slope of her breast. Rafe lifted his head just enough so that his mouth hovered directly above her breast. She could feel his breath on her skin. Expectation was replaced with raw excitement as he set her ablaze with a stroke of his tongue, wetting the silk of her bra and then blowing on the damp material.

Steeped in passion, Jenny didn't even know where she was anymore. And she didn't care. The only important thing was Rafe and the ecstasy he was promising her. His hands were reaching for the front fastening of her bra and he was about to lower his head to kiss her once more. . . .

"North Dunway police," a voice shouted. "Freeze!"

Chapter Eight

'Come on. Stand up real nice and slow,'' the policeman ordered Rafe. "No sudden moves. Keep your hands on top of your head.''

With a muttered string of soft curses, Rafe glared down into Jenny's eyes, holding her personally responsible for his current predicament. For the time being he had no choice but to do what the cop ordered; however, his expression promised retribution for Jenny later. "Why didn't you tell me you hit the alarm?'' he muttered under his breath in exasperation.

"Stand up. Now!'' the cop barked.

"Look, I'm her husband,'' Rafe said as he obeyed the policemen's curt order.

The cop just said, "Keep your hands where I can see them.''

"I'm not the reason she called you, dammit!''

"Calm down, Rafe,'' Jenny said, scrambling to her feet and hastily rebuttoning her blouse. "I'm Jenny Benjamin.''

"Murphy," Rafe inserted. "Jenny Murphy."

"Right. Jenny Benjamin-Murphy. The important thing is that I'm the one who hit the security alarm," Jenny told the police officer. "There was someone outside, an intruder. I didn't see him very clearly, just a shadowy outline. My husband arrived and scared the intruder away before could get a better look at him."

"Sure, blame things on me," Rafe said with a glare in her direction.

"Do you have any ID, sir?" a second policeman inquired.

Rafe nodded. "I own Murphy's, the restaurant next door."

"I don't eat out much," the cop replied. "I'll need to see that ID. You too, ma'am."

Rafe showed it to him, taking care to remove his wallet from his back pocket with slow and easy movements before pulling out his driver's license.

"I don't have any ID on me right now," Jenny said. "I left my purse at home. I live right next door."

"I'll vouch for her," Rafe stated.

Jenny wasn't amused by his superior tone of voice and her gaze told him so.

"All right." The police officer returned his gun to its holster and Rafe's driver's license back to Rafe. Nodding to his partner, who'd stood quietly in the background all this time, he said, "Bert here will check around outside and see if he can find anything." The policeman then turned away to speak into his hand-held radio.

While the officers were otherwise occupied, Rafe took the opportunity to speak to Jenny privately. "I can't believe you did that!" Rafe muttered softly, his dark blue eyes shooting fire at her. "Why didn't you tell me that you'd hit the silent alarm for the cops?"

"You didn't give me a chance," Jenny retorted. "You were too busy bawling me out for coming over here to work."

"It was a stupid thing to do."

"Working in my own building, which has a security system is not something I'd call stupid. Getting caught by the police necking with your wife, however . . . now that might qualify."

"Why didn't you tell them right away who I was?" Without giving her a chance to reply, Rafe answered his question himself. "You did that on purpose, didn't you?"

"You're absolutely right, Rafe," Jenny shot back in a sugary voice dripping with sarcasm. "After hitting the alarm I decided I'd thoroughly embarrass you and myself by getting into a compromising situation before the police came. So I seduced you against your will and forced you down onto that couch. I admit it. There. I hope you're happy now."

He was not amused by her mocking retort. She could see that. Well, tough toenails, she thought to herself. She wasn't real pleased with him at the moment, either.

The two of them glared at each other in a visual shoot-out that was interrupted by the return of the policeman named Bert.

"Not much to see outside," Bert reported. "There are several sets of footprints, nothing distinct."

"I'm sure there was someone out there," Jenny insisted. "I saw him."

"What did he look like?" the first police officer asked, opening his notebook and standing with pencil poised.

"I couldn't see his face," Jenny admitted. "But he was shorter than Rafe. And he was acting very furtive. It looked like he might have been dressed in black. He didn't look overweight—average build I'd say."

"What makes you think it was a man?" the officer asked.

"The way he walked," she replied.

"Any idea of age?"

Jenny shook her head. "I couldn't see his hair, but it didn't appear to be white or anything. Actually he may have been wearing a dark stocking cap or something like that. tried to get a better look at him, but my husband stormed in and scared the intruder away." She gave Rafe a meaningful look.

"Did you see anything?" the cop asked Rafe.

"No."

"Mind if I ask why you were storming over here?" the officer continued.

"I was worried about my wife," Rafe replied.

"Oh? And why's that?"

"It was getting late and she hadn't come home yet," Rafe explained.

"Ever heard of using the phone?" Jenny retorted.

Rafe glared at her, not wanting to admit that he'd been so concerned when she still wasn't back by ten at night that the option of using the phone hadn't even occurred to him.

"Any particular reason why you were concerned about your wife?" the officer asked Rafe.

"She's had some trouble over here before," Rafe said.

The investigating officer turned his attention back to Jenny. "So this isn't the first time you've had trouble like this?"

"No," Jenny had to admit. "There have been several other incidences, although this is the first time I've actually spotted someone."

"What kind of incidences?" the officer asked.

"Small things in the beginning. The most serious was the hole in my roof. Mr. Fadden, the contractor I got to fix it told me that he thought the hole was made deliberately. But then Mr. Gardner apparently isn't the best contractor in the world. He was the contractor I had before Mr. Fadden," she added parenthetically. "Anyway, I didn't get suspicious until the incident at the bank. Then I knew that MegaToys was behind everything."

"MegaToys?" the policeman replied, trying to keep up.

Jenny nodded. "That's right. You see, I make teddy bears. And when I refused to sell out to MegaToys, they got angry. So they've started this campaign to make sure my company doesn't succeed."

The cop looked skeptical, to put it mildly.

"Listen, Officer, I can assure you that this is a serious matter," Jenny stated.

Rafe was amused to note the way her hands automatically headed for her hips, a sure sign she was getting aggravated.

"Right, ma'am. Do you have any proof that MegaToys is behind the trouble? Any witnesses to someone making this hole in your roof?"

"No. And no one saw the guys who snuck into my house a few weeks ago and stole several designs, either," she retorted in irritation.

"You're saying someone broke into your home? Did you report it with us then?" the officer asked.

"No," Jenny admitted.

"Listen, the barn door was open when I got here," Rafe inserted, almost forgetting that point in the subsequent mayhem.

"Studio," Jenny automatically corrected him. "This is my studio now. Not a barn. Not anymore. And I'm sure I locked the door when Miriam left around six."

"Hey, I think I found something," Bert called out from the shadowy interior of the studio.

He was in the far side of the building, the farthest from Jenny's office, an area she couldn't actually see at all from her work space. It was the shipping area, where newly completed bears were awaiting shipping out to their new owners.

Rafe got there first. "No, Jenny, don't...." He put his arm around her as if to shield her from the view.

She had to see. Bracing herself, she leaned around him.

Five bears had been waiting shipment...and three of them had been torn apart. Cut apart, actually as if with some kind of very sharp instrument.

Jenny got a sudden vision of the Scarecrow from *The Wizard of Oz* when the meanies had pulled his straw stuffing out. The Scarecrow had recovered. These bears wouldn't. Tears welled in her eyes. How could someone do this to teddy bears, a universal symbol of friendship and love? She shivered.

Rafe tightened his arm around her, keeping her close by his side.

Once the original shock wore off, Jenny's pain was followed by fury. It was one thing to trash her roof and even to break into her house, but harming her bears was something else. The culprits, whomever they were, had gone too far this time! Now she was really shaking with the force of her emotions.

Rafe felt her shivering intensify. He tried to reassure her and calm her down by rubbing his hand up and down her arm, but his own emotions were seething, because he didn't think this incident had anything to do with industrial sabotage. They had to be dealing with some kind of weirdo here—a weirdo that had been in the building alone with Jenny. The damage done to her bears was deliberate, and the shock on Jenny's face ate at him. But she could have ended up the way her teddy bears had, and that fact ate at him even more.

For Jenny, the next hour was a blur. More police officers came and went, something to do with checking for fingerprints. Jenny stayed in her office until they were done, answering questions, filling in forms and mourning her lost bears.

They also got a locksmith out to change the locks and the code on the security alarm. While overseeing the locksmith's work, Rafe broodingly reflected on the night's events. One thing had become very clear to him. Jenny had gotten under his skin and was threatening to lodge herself in his heart. It shook him to discover how important she'd become to him in such a relatively short period of time.

"There's nothing more you can do here tonight," Rafe told Jenny after the locksmith had finally left. Placing both hands palm down on her desk, he leaned forward to give her one of his dark and brooding stares. "Don't you dare pull something like this again. How am I supposed to look after you when you take off on your own?" Rafe demanded, the scare he'd gotten making him curt with her.

"I didn't take off. I was right here, working."

"Late at night. By yourself."

"In a building that was supposed to be locked with a security system. A building that happens to be right next door to your restaurant."

"What's that supposed to mean? Are you accusing me of having something to do with this?"

"No. You don't have to bite off my head every time I say anything. I just meant that it's not like I was out in the middle of no place. And if you hadn't stormed in here yelling at me tonight, then we'd have caught whoever is behind this."

"And maybe you'd have ended up slashed the way your bears were," Rafe shot back. "Did you ever stop to consider that?"

"I'm not going to let these people scare me away," she stated quietly. "I'm not going to let them win."

"This isn't a matter of winning. It's a matter of your safety."

"Which is why I had that security system installed, although it doesn't seem to have done a heck of a lot. My poor bears." Jenny bit her lip, determined not to cry in front of him.

"I've already seen you cry, you know," he pointed out.

Jenny didn't appreciate being reminded of the fact. "I want to know how he got in here," she stated angrily.

"You probably forgot to lock the door after Miriam left."

"I did not forget!"

"Jenny, you forget what time it is," he noted in exasperation. "You've said yourself that when you're working you lose track of things."

"I didn't lose track of locking the door," she maintained.

"How can you be sure?"

She couldn't, not positively, and she wasn't pleased with him for making her doubt herself this way. *She* was the one who had cause to be angry, not Rafe. And she couldn't just stand around doing nothing. She couldn't go back to his house and pretend this hadn't happened, either. She had to take action, or go crazy. "I'm moving the rest of my bears into the house and then I'm going to stay there and protect them," Jenny decided.

"No, you're not. The police have said they'll have a squad car cruise this area throughout the night."

"They won't be able to stop that guy if he comes back."

"Neither will you."

"I'm not going to leave my bears unprotected."

"They're not unprotected. You've got a security system."

"That didn't work before."

"Don't be ridiculous. There's no way I'm allowing you to risk your life for a few stupid teddy bears," he growled.

That did it! Jenny's control snapped. "You can't tell me what's important in my life," she yelled at him.

"What about your life itself? How much good are those bears going to be if you're killed?"

She ignored him, and instead gathered up as many of her bears as she could in a large container she kept for such a purpose—a wicker trunk of sorts. She still had her bears out on the display tables from the grand opening.

Moving closer, Rafe happened to see the price tag on one of her original-artist bears and his jaw dropped.

"They're expensive to make," Jenny informed him. "A yard of quality synthetic material can cost from twenty to eighty dollars. Mohair runs anywhere from seventy to a hundred-and-thirty a yard."

"And people buy them at this price?"

"I'm here, aren't I?" she retorted in irritation. "With a business that's doing quite well when it's not being sabotaged. Besides, I don't tell you that you charge too much for your dinners, do I?"

"No."

"Then don't tell me I charge too much for my bears. These are collector's items. I guess you'd have to be a bear collector to understand."

"I can understand seeing something and wanting it, despite what it might cost you." His gaze was brooding and filled with emotions and hidden messages that Jenny desperately wanted to decipher but was unable to.

With an effort, Jenny looked away and finished packing her bears while Rafe looked on, making her feel very self-conscious. Consequently, her voice was curt as she said, "Are you going to help me or not?"

Muttering under his breath, Rafe took the now filled trunk from her.

"It takes two people to carry it," she warned him.

"If you're a weakling maybe," he retorted, ignoring her attempts to help him.

"Right. I wouldn't want to deprive you of a chance to show off your macho abilities," Jenny retorted sarcastically, locking the studio and activating the alarm before hurrying to unlock her house. Once Rafe had deposited the trunk in the dining room, sliding it under the table at her request, she accompanied him to her back door. "Thanks. I'll see you in the morning."

"That's right. You're gonna see me tonight, too."

She shot him a startled look. "There's no need for you to stay here."

"No need for *you* to stay here, either. And you're not," he stated.

It did strike Jenny as ironic that here they were, having come full circle, arguing on her back steps again as they had that very first night. Then she'd only had a hint of the temptation and havoc Rafe could create in her life. But that embrace they'd shared in her office had changed everything. Now she *knew* what he could do to her, how he made her feel, how he made her forget, made her want things she couldn't have, made her even think she loved him. She needed some time to herself to get things back into perspective.

So many things had changed since that first night. Her feelings for Rafe, the fact that they were now husband and wife. Even the rickety steps themselves had been reinforced by Mr. Fadden. Right now Jenny had to concentrate on reinforcing her own defenses.

"I'm staying here tonight, Rafe."

"No way."

Jenny hated to be given orders. "What did you say?"

"No way. And I'm not just saying it, I'll show you what I mean." Without further ado, Rafe took the keys from her hand and picked her up in a fireman's lift over his shoulder. Ignoring her indignant shriek, Rafe juggled her against his shoulder as he locked the door before carrying her down the steps.

"You're crazy," she shouted as she hung upside down.

He ignored her and kept walking, so fast that she had to hang on to something or keep bouncing against his back. She grabbed hold of the belt loops on his jeans. Not wanting to wake Cindy, Jenny kept her protests to a low growl as Rafe carried her through the back entrance, past a startled Spud who was just finishing the cleaning up, to the stairs leading to their private quarters.

Rafe had just rounded the first landing and was heading for the next flight of stairs leading to their third-floor master bedroom when he got close enough to the living room doorway for Jenny to grab hold of it with both hands. *That* stopped him in his tracks, she thought with some satisfaction.

From down the hallway, Cindy said, "What are you doing? Is something wrong?"

Seeing the little girl's look of concern, Jenny stopped struggling—without releasing her hold on the door frame, however—and pasted a reassuring smile on her face. "Nothing is wrong. Your daddy is just playing a game. He's pretending to be a brainless caveman."

"And she's pretending to be a flighty female," Rafe growled.

"Can I play? Can I?" Cindy asked.

"Sure," Jenny said. "Your daddy was just about to put me down, weren't you, Rafe?"

With his daughter right there, there wasn't much Rafe could do but obey. Muttering a soft oath, Rafe slid her off his shoulder. Jenny had to lean against the door frame a moment as she readjusted to being upright again.

"What are you doing up so late, kiddo?" Rafe turned to ask Cindy with a frown. "It's way past your bedtime."

"I couldn't sleep."

"Did you have a bad dream?" Rafe asked in concern.

"No. I couldn't sleep 'cause I forgot to ask Jenny something. I waited up, but you didn't come home for dinner."

"I'm sorry about that," Jenny said softly. "The bears kept me busy and just wouldn't let me go," she added in an attempt to make Cindy feel better, knowing the little girl related to Jenny's bears as if they were real. "What did you want to ask me?"

"Can I bring you to school as my show-'n'-tell thing?" Cindy said. "Our teacher said we can bring anything we want to show off and I wanted to show off my new mommy."

Jenny swallowed a lump in her throat, and stole a look at Rafe to see what his reaction was to Cindy's words. But he was wearing his stoic face, the one that didn't allow her to see anything of what he was feeling.

"Will you come tomorrow?" Cindy asked Jenny. "And bring some teddy bears with you? That would be...impressive."

"Tomorrow? That's not much time to prepare."

"I was gonna ask you before, only I forgot 'til today. That's okay, right? You'll still be my show-'n'-tell thing even though I forgot, right?"

"I've never been a show-'n'-tell thing before," Jenny replied with a smile.

"You don't have to be nervous," Cindy assured her. Leaning forward, she confidentially told her, "If you throw up, the teacher won't yell."

"How reassuring," Jenny noted wryly.

"I know 'cause we had someone throw up today and Mrs. Kent didn't yell," Cindy added. "So, will you come?"

"Sure, I will."

"Come on, kiddo. Back to bed for you," Rafe said.

While Rafe was busy tucking in Cindy, Jenny made her getaway. She was tempted to slip off and go back home, and probably would have had it not been for the sure knowledge that Rafe would simply have followed her and pounded on her door until he woke the entire neighborhood.

So she reluctantly headed upstairs and got ready for bed, all the while mentally preparing herself for a head-on argument with Rafe, because she wasn't about to allow him to think he could get away with treating her the way he had. The only problem with her plan was that Rafe didn't show up. In fact, she fell asleep waiting for him.

Chapter Nine

Jenny woke to the muffled sound of an engine droning in her ear and the uneasy feeling that someone was watching her. Rafe?

She opened her eyes to find a pair of greeny-yellow cat eyes staring at her. "Boots, what are you doing up here?" Jenny sleepily asked the cat.

And then it all came back to her. She'd woken up at three as a result of a bad nightmare—all about her bears getting hurt and Rafe walking away from her—and she'd been so shaken as a result that she hadn't been able to get back to sleep. So she'd sneaked downstairs to get the can of chocolate frosting she'd bought and hidden in Rafe's tiny kitchen cupboards, way in the back. Grabbing a spoon, she'd turned to head back upstairs, and ended up almost tripping over Boots, who was twining around her ankles.

The gray-and-white cat had looked up at Jenny with such big "pet me" eyes that Jenny had given in and picked the cat up, carrying her upstairs with her. Boots had purred and settled on the bed to wash herself while Jenny polished off half the can of chocolate frosting in one sitting.

Jenny had seen no sign of Rafe during her postmidnight raid. He hadn't come to bed at all last night. At least not *this* bed. There was still the guest bedroom downstairs, she reminded herself. The one he'd shared with Susan.

"Thanks for keeping me company last night, Boots," Jenny murmured, scratching the cat under her chin for a special reward.

Boots closed her eyes and purred in ecstasy.

While petting the cat, Jenny reflected back on that heated embrace last night she and Rafe had shared on the couch in her office. And the realization that there was more at work here than just physical attraction. Jenny was scared to the bottom of her soul that she'd fallen in love with Rafe, despite her best efforts not to do so. For while she was afraid she loved him, she was *sure* he didn't love her. How could he when his heart had been buried with his dead wife?

Oh, he might want Jenny, he might find her attractive, but he didn't feel for her what she felt for him. And she had to decide what to do about it. What *could* she do? Sure, a woman with moxie would go after Rafe, would try her darnedest to make him fall in love with her. But Jenny was seriously beginning to doubt she was a woman with moxie after all. At the moment she felt more like a *schlemazel,* someone for whom nothing was going right, someone with no luck at all.

After showering and washing her hair, Jenny felt a little better. Remembering her promise to show up at Cindy's kindergarten class, Jenny decided she'd better wear something casual today. So, to boost her confidence, she put on one of her favorite outfits—black slacks and her chenille turtleneck sweater in blue scattered with flecks of other colors. The sweater was a long tunic length. It was also the outfit she'd worn when she'd gone on that picnic with Rafe. What she'd worn the first time he'd ever kissed her.

Maybe she should change? Changing clothes wouldn't change the way she felt, Jenny realized with a sigh. Might as well face the bogeyman head-on. Taking a deep breath, she headed downstairs, ready to face Rafe.

The living room was empty. She let out the breath she didn't know she'd been holding, telling herself she'd be better able to handle Rafe once she'd had some toast and coffee. She'd finished the toast and was on her second cup of coffee when she realized that Boots, who'd eaten a breakfast of dried cat food, had jumped onto the beige couch and gone back to sleep again.

Jenny sat down next to the snoozing feline. The cat had such soft fur, she noted as she ran her hand over the cat's back. And Boots had perfect features. She looked as if an artist had taken the all gray cat and added white on her four paws, a bib under her chest and a streak up from her nose. Jenny was considering the possibility of adding cats to her collection, making a few mental designs, when her thoughts were interrupted by the sound of a man's voice.

"I don't believe that cat's sleeping again," Chuck noted as he entered the living room.

"I remember reading somewhere that cats spend up to two thirds of their lives sleeping."

"That does it, then. In my next life, I'm coming back as a house cat," Chuck stated.

Jenny smiled, while unobtrusively looking past Chuck to see if Rafe was with him. She apparently wasn't as unobtrusive as she'd hoped, because Chuck said, "Rafe's not here. He had some trouble to work out with a vendor and some supplies to pick up, errands to run—that kind of thing."

"You don't have to cover for him," Jenny said.

The older man sighed. "There's no use me pretending that I don't know you two had a fight last night," he said.

"Did Rafe talk to you about it?"

"Of course not. But I've got ears in my head. I heard you two coming upstairs last night. Saw you dangling over his shoulder and you didn't look none too pleased about it, either."

"I wasn't. I'm still not."

"That why Rafe slept in the guest bedroom last night?"

So Jenny's earlier suspicions were correct. He had slept in the room he'd shared with Susan. It didn't help ease the onslaught of pain any. "You'd have to ask him that question," she said. "I wouldn't dream of attempting to read his mind. It would be impossible to get through that thick skull of his anyway."

"Don't you see?" Chuck said. "Rafe's acting this way because he *does* care about you. If he weren't so darned afraid of what he's feeling, he'd be happy and cheerful, not acting like a bear with a toothache."

"You're telling me that Rafe is acting like a maniac because of me? Am I making him that unhappy?" She was stricken at the very idea.

"Not at all. Well, you may be keeping him up nights..." Chuck actually blushed. "That is... I'm not trying to butt into your business, believe me," he hurried on to say. "I just thought maybe you could use a few... I don't know." He scratched his head. "Pointers, maybe, on how to deal with my son. I realize he may not be the easiest guy in the world to figure out."

"You can say that again. And I'd appreciate any insight you could give me into his attitude."

"Don't misunderstand me. I love my son. Raised him right, too. He's worked hard to get where he is. Nobody handed him anything on a silver platter. He's had to work for everything he wanted. But there's no getting around the fact that Susan's death changed him, made him tougher.''

"I already know that he loved her very much," Jenny whispered, getting the words past a throat that felt as if it had a fist clenched around it.

"Rafe was in bad shape after Susan died. Those were tough times for him. Real tough. It almost destroyed him when she died.''

Jenny looked away, fighting off the tears. She didn't want to hear this. It only made the pain worse.

"Rafe didn't want to fall in love again," Chuck said bluntly. "But clearly he has. With you.''

Jenny stared at Chuck in amazement. "It doesn't look that clear from where I'm standing.''

"He married you, didn't he?''

Jenny nodded. Sure, to many that would be proof of a man's love, proof of his desire for a commitment. But that wasn't the case with Rafe, not that she could tell Chuck that.

"And that's not all," Chuck continued. "I've seen the way he looks at you.''

"How does he look at me?" Jenny couldn't resist asking.

"The way Hugo eyes those fancy foreign catalogs with the latest cooking paraphernalia from Europe. With hunger.''

Which only proved that Rafe might want her, not that he loved her, Jenny silently noted.

"And then there's his behavior," Chuck added. "As I said earlier, Rafe is upset because he's fallen for you and he didn't want to. Because he doesn't want to go through what he went through when he lost Susan.''

Part of Jenny couldn't blame Rafe for that. She hadn't wanted to love him for the same reason, not wanting to go through the pain and the barren loss of having him desert her the way her father had. But she wasn't sure she bought Chuck's interpretation of Rafe's behavior. Rafe could also be acting like a bear with a toothache because he regretted marrying her, because he felt guilty about wanting to take her to bed when his heart still belonged to Susan.

"Just think about the possibility that Rafe is acting the way he is because he cares for you. Can you do that much?" Chuck asked. "And be patient with him."

"I don't know about being patient with him. He'd try the patience of a saint, and I'm no saint. But I will think about what you've said, Chuck. And thank you for taking the time to talk to me. I appreciate it."

"Bah!" Chuck self-consciously waved away her gratitude, before giving her a hug. "You're family now. It's the least I can do. Just don't tell Rafe what a buttinsky I was, okay?"

"I wouldn't dream of it," Jenny assured him.

"Hank, you go first and then Cindy can do her show-and-tell," Mrs. Kent, the kindergarten teacher said.

"I brought Ben for my show-'n'-tell," Hank said as he got in front of the class.

Sitting in the back of the classroom, Jenny was expecting maybe a hamster or at worst a snake. Instead, Ben turned out to be a doll. Looking around at the other kids in the class, she realized no one seemed the least bit taken aback and there was no snickering going on.

"Ben's gonna help me be a good daddy someday," Hank stated proudly. "I used to practice on my new baby sister but I almost dropped her so my mommy got me Ben to practice on. Now, when my daddy has to diaper my baby sister's smelly diapers, I get to diaper Ben, and his diapers aren't nearly as smelly as my sister's. So I'm gonna show you how to diaper, 'cause it's not that easy. You have to be smart."

As Jenny listened to Hank's earnest presentation, she thought how great it was that some of the sexist stereotypes were being broken down before they could get started, and that parenting skills were being valued at such a young age. Maybe if her own father had been shown how important fatherhood was, things might have been different.

Jenny's gaze settled on Cindy. Rafe knew how important fatherhood was—so important that he'd married a woman he didn't love in order to keep his daughter. While Jenny was still resistant to the idea of loving Rafe, she had accepted the fact that she'd grown to love Cindy. But Jenny was new to parenthood and still nervous of making a mistake.

Cindy showed no such qualms as she confidently stood in front of the class and began her presentation. "Jenny used to be my friend. Now she's my mommy. And she makes teddy bears. And she's famous. And I'm glad she's my new mommy. She's gonna tell you about teddy bears now."

With that intro, Cindy sat down and Jenny stood. Opening the large duffel bag she'd brought with her, she pulled out the bears one at a time, feeling rather like a magician pulling rabbits out of the proverbial hat. She'd brought several bears with her, in various sizes. She started with the smallest ones, four inches high.

"Like people, teddy bears come in all colors, shapes and sizes. From little chubby ones like this fellow, to skinnier, taller ones like this one."

Jenny had debated over whether or not to go into a thumbnail history of teddy bears, including the fact that they got their name from a political cartoon about President Teddy Roosevelt's hunting trip back in the early 1900's. But she decided against that rather quickly. After all, these were five-year-olds here, not known for their extended attention span.

Instead she decided to focus on the good bears could do. "You know, teddy bears are great listeners," Jenny said. "You can tell them all your secrets, knowing they'll never tell anyone else. All a teddy bear really needs is a lot of love—at least two hugs a day is good.''

Because small hands could be curious and her artist bears weren't made for children—in fact, since most of her bears didn't have safety eyes, they carried a notice, at her attorney's suggestion, that they were collectibles and not intended for small children—she hadn't brought any of her original designs along. But she had brought along one of her popular wool tweed Grandfather Bears, because he did have safety eyes. The children seemed to get a kick out of the bear's spectacles.

Handing Grandfather Bear around, she said, ''Grandfather Bear is getting older, so he needs to wear his glasses although he complains about it all the time.''

''My grandpa does that, too,'' a little boy piped up. ''He's always losing his glasses, too.''

''Well, Grandfather Bear used to lose his, until I sewed them on for him. Not that I'd recommend that with your grandfather,'' Jenny hastily added, just in case any of the imaginative five-year-olds got any ideas!

Next, Jenny passed around several pictures of her clothed bears she'd had taken by a professional photographer. ''These are some of the bears I've made. They had to stay home today, but Grandfather Bear came along to show you what my bears look like.''

Since Jenny had put some clothes on the commercial bears she'd brought along, they were a big hit.

''Doctors like teddy bears, too,'' Jenny added. ''They even use them in the hospital to make their patients feel better.'' In fact, Jenny knew several pediatricians and even psychologists who used bears in the course of their treatment. In addition, police officers and emergency medical technicians in ambulances always had a teddy bear on board should they come across a traumatized child. She'd donated a few commercial bears for that cause herself.

"When my dad was in the hospital for his heart operation, they gave him a teddy bear to hold and to cough with," one little girl piped up. "He even got to bring it home with him."

"Well, all of you are going to be able to bring Grandfather Bear home with you for a night if you'd like to," Jenny said. "Mrs. Kent has agreed to make a home for Grandfather Bear here in your class and you'll be allowed to take him home overnight, providing you write a story about him and bring it back with you the next morning. You see, Grandfather Bear is getting a little older, and I'm afraid he might forget things," Jenny confessed with a smile. "That's why he needs you children to write down his life story for him." Jenny had checked this out with Mrs. Kent beforehand and the teacher had agreed enthusiastically with the plan. "And all the stories you write can go together into a book about Grandfather Bear done by your class."

This idea was greeted with a great deal of approval from the kids.

"I think you're lucky to have a mom like that," Jenny overheard a little girl enviously telling Cindy, who grinned and nodded her agreement. Now, Jenny wistfully noted, if only Rafe were to feel the same way—about having her for a *wife* and not just as a mother for his daughter.

"So how did the show-and-tell go?" Miriam asked as Jenny entered the studio later that afternoon. "Looks like you survived being in a roomful of kindergartners. They give you a medal?"

"It wasn't that bad, Miriam."

"Of course it wasn't. Being pinned, naked, to an anthill with honey spread all over you—now that's bad. A roomful of rowdy five-year-olds is just mildly distressful."

"They weren't all that rowdy, and you'd be amazed at how those five-year-olds have changed from when we were in kindergarten."

"Changed how?"

"Well, for example, one of the little boys brought a doll to class for his show-and-tell. No one blinked an eye. And the boy bragged about how he was learning to diaper his doll just like his daddy was diapering his baby sister."

"There may be hope for the next generation, after all," Miriam decided.

"Well, meanwhile let's concentrate on the here and now. Did the insurance claims adjuster show up while I was gone?"

Miriam nodded. "He seemed a little suspicious about two claims coming so close together. First the roof and now this."

"It's more than suspicious, it's criminal. I can't believe the police have my damaged bears as evidence."

"I can't believe someone got in here last night."

"I locked the door after you left last night, Miriam. I know I did."

"I know you did, too. I heard the lock click."

"Thank heavens!" Jenny hugged her. "A witness that I'm not losing my mind."

"What are you talking about?"

"I was sure I'd locked the door, but Rafe said it was open when he got here last night. He made me think that I'd screwed up and somehow forgotten to lock it. But then I can't think straight when he's around, period," Jenny muttered.

"So I've heard. Max tells me that he heard via the grapevine that the police arrived to find you and Rafe making out in your office."

"Great," Jenny muttered. "Does the entire town know about it?"

"Not yet maybe."

Jenny groaned.

Miriam nodded her agreement. "I know. It's a sad thing. What is this country coming to when a person can't make out with her own husband without the police breaking it up." Her grin belied her solemn tone of voice.

"That's not why the police came. They were here because I hit the silent alarm."

"Before or after you and Rafe hit the couch?"

"Before. He made me forget...."

"*Oy*, I know how that can go! Even after thirty years, Max can still make me forget," Miriam noted with a satisfied gleam in her eyes.

When Jenny didn't say anything, Miriam keenly picked up on her silence. "So what's bothering you? That you got caught by the police making out with your husband?"

"No."

"Something is wrong. And don't try blaming it on what happened to your bears. Something else is bothering you, too."

"Having someone cut up my bears isn't enough to bother me?" Jenny countered.

"It's more than enough. But there's still something else. Did you and Rafe have an argument?"

"He tossed me over his shoulder and forcibly removed me from my own back steps. I'd call that more than an argument."

"My goodness. He tossed you over his shoulder? Max only did that to me once, way back when we were newlyweds. I disgraced myself by emptying the contents of my stomach. It took the romance out of the moment, you know?"

"The man is a Neanderthal," Jenny stated.

"Well, I wouldn't say that. I think Max was entitled to get upset. After all, it *was* his favorite shirt."

"I'm talking about Rafe. He doesn't understand how important my bears are to me. He doesn't understand how much I hate being ordered around. He just plain doesn't understand me." Not to mention him not loving me, Jenny silently added.

"Did you ever think maybe he acted so badly because he was worried about you? You know men act very strangely when they get scared."

"So I've been told."

"Had Rafe said he didn't care what happened to you or that you could stay on your back steps for two decades, then you should be worried. What were you two doing on your back steps anyway?"

"I'd just taken my bears into the house. Well, actually Rafe carried them in the wicker trunk. Then I hid the trunk under the dining room table, just in case someone should go looking for them. They should be safe. The tablecloth hanging down covers it so you can't see anything is under there, and the house does have a security system. Not that my faith has been restored in security systems after what happened last night."

Miriam shook her head in disbelief. "What kind of person would want to destroy teddy bears?"

"MegaToys was sending me a clear message. They're obviously prepared to pay hardball. Well, so am I," Jenny vowed. "And whoever is responsible is going to pay."

The first time Jenny saw Rafe since their argument was at dinner that night. He was as closemouthed as ever and as brooding. Cindy was a veritable chatterbox as she excitedly recited the events of her show-and-tell event of the day. To give him credit, Rafe patiently listened to every replay Cindy told him.

While his attention was taken up with his daughter, Jenny took the opportunity to study Rafe. Why had she had to go and fall in love with him? What was it about him that got to her? So he had a wonderfully sculpted pair of lips that could kiss like nobody else on the face of this earth. That was no reason for her to go off the deep end.

And, okay, so he was a great father. She'd known that from the beginning and she'd still managed to avoid falling for him. Or had she just been kidding herself all along? Jenny uneasily wondered. Had she been telling herself she was merely attracted to him when in fact she'd already started feeling much more?

Jenny didn't know. She only knew that she was stuck now. And panicked about it. Because Rafe showed no signs of feeling the same way she did.

It should be enough that she was part of a family, that Cindy and Chuck had accepted her with open arms, Jenny admonished herself. She had a roof over her head . . . well, three of them actually—her house, her studio and Rafe's house. And food on her table—not just plain fare but gourmet meals like *boeuf bourguignon, coq au vin, filets de sole* with a lemon sauce that melted in your mouth, and even lobster thermidor. That wasn't so hard to take, surely? Jenny told herself that she should be looking on the bright side of the situation instead of moping.

Her self-lecture didn't do much to lift her spirits as Rafe continued to basically ignore her. After dinner, he retreated to his office—a room Jenny hadn't even seen and didn't even know the location of. Somewhere on the first floor. The house was actually large enough to qualify for mansion status. Victorians liked having plenty of room.

That evening, Jenny fussed over Cindy, redoing her nails for her, overseeing her bath and tucking her into bed, reading her *Sleeping Beauty*, all without Rafe who remained holed up in his office, working on the end of the month accounting—or so Chuck informed her.

By midnight, the strain got too much for Jenny, who'd gone to bed but not to sleep. Getting up, she tugged on a pair of well-worn jeans and her softest flannel shirt. She needed to get out, get some fresh air. Realizing it was chilly outside, she added a jean jacket before slipping downstairs.

There was no light from under the guest bedroom door, which was closed, so Jenny didn't know if Rafe had gone to bed there or if he was still working in his office. Either way, she didn't want to face him. She needed soothing, not arguing. A short walk should relax her. She wouldn't go far, just around the house.

While not as bright as when it had been full, the moon still provided enough light for Jenny to see by as she followed the path leading from the back door around to the front of Murphy's. Most of the leaves had fallen from the trees now, and crunched under her feet. The branches were bare, mere skeletal dark outlines against the luminous sky. Jenny shivered, not only because of the crisp night air but because of the sudden loneliness that enveloped her.

Sticking her hands in the pockets of her jean jacket, Jenny decided that while she was outside, she might as well mosey on over and check on her studio, just to make sure everything was okay. Things seemed quiet, and she was about to walk away when she heard something. A rustling of leaves.

Jenny froze, realizing too late that taking a midnight walk with an intruder still on the loose might not have been the brightest thing she'd ever done. She was about to scream when a raccoon came waddling around the corner. So that was the noise she'd heard.

Jenny sagged with relief. Talk about being spooked! She was seeing trouble where there was none.

Still with this much adrenaline racing through her system, she'd never get to sleep now. She might as well pick up some work while she was this close. Jenny wouldn't stay in the studio, but would just pick up that antique silk doll's dress she was adapting for a new Bambino Bear she was working on. She'd probably be able to finish it tonight. Heaven knew, it didn't look like she'd be getting much rest at this rate, she noted while deactivating the security system.

Jenny barely took two steps inside before she realized her mistake. She wasn't alone in the studio. Someone else was there! It wasn't Rafe—she sensed that instinctively. There was danger here, real danger.

She whirled to leave, but before she could move, she was grabbed from behind, the intruder ruthlessly placing a rough hand over her mouth to prevent her from screaming.

Chapter Ten

Jenny had taken off again. This time Rafe was going to do more than just toss her over his shoulder, he silently vowed as his long legs ate up the short distance between his place and hers. This time he'd teach her a lesson she'd never forget.

Instead, he walked in on a scene *he'd* never forget—Jenny fighting off a ski-masked intruder.

Jenny didn't know what happened—one minute she was struggling to get loose from the frantic hold the intruder had on her. The next second she was free and Rafe was there, smashing a fist into the guy's face as he used the street-fighting techniques he must have picked up as a teenager.

The masked intruder was no match for Rafe, and the battle was over shortly after it began with the man in a boneless heap at Rafe's feet.

"Are you all right?" Rafe rushed to Jenny's side to ask. Smoothing her disheveled hair away from her face, he anxiously checked her features for any sign of an injury.

"I'm fine," she shakily assured him, welcoming the feel of his arms around her. "He didn't hurt me."

When the intruder groaned and showed signs of regaining consciousness, Rafe released Jenny and leaned down to yank off the guy's ski mask.

"Mr. Gardner!" Jenny exclaimed. For an instant she wondered if they'd made a mistake in attacking the contractor. "What were you doing in my studio?"

"You still owe me money," the contractor said, shaking his head as if attempting to clear his senses.

"So you broke into my studio to get it?" Jenny demanded in disbelief.

"Call the police, Jenny," Rafe curtly ordered her. "Gardner can make his explanations to them."

"There's no need to involve the police in this," Mr. Gardner protested.

Lifting the man up by the front of his shirt, Rafe gave him an icy look of rage. "There's every need to involve the police. You attacked my wife. That's assault and battery. Consider yourself lucky I didn't do more than rearrange that ugly face of yours."

When Gardner started struggling against the hold Rafe had on him, Rafe quickly subdued him and ordered Jenny, who was just hanging up from calling the police, to find him something to tie the contractor up with. Acting with quickminded cleverness, she grabbed an extension cord from the wall and handed it to Rafe.

Once Gardner was safely trussed up, the man started trying to plea-bargain. "Look, this wasn't my idea. Rafe, you know me. I'm not a hardened criminal. I may have cut a few corners at times...."

"You attacked my wife."

"I didn't know who she was. She scared me. I wasn't thinking clearly."

"You can say that again," Rafe agreed. "You're gonna regret this day for the rest of your life, Gardner. I can promise you that."

"I needed the money."

"And who paid you? MegaToys?" Jenny demanded.

"I could get into trouble for saying."

"You don't think you're in trouble already?" Rafe inquired over the wail of a police siren.

Gardner got pale, his eyes darting from side to side. "No one said anything about getting arrested. The people at MegaToys told me it would be simple. Just scare her off so she couldn't get the company started."

Jenny moved closer to stare down at him. "So you admit that you were the one who made those phone calls, screwed up my delivery schedule . . . and the worse thing of all—you broke my bears' arms! Chopped them up!"

Jenny was so furious, she looked ready to break Mr. Gardner's arms, Rafe noted with admiration and a touch of amusement. Rafe also noted that Gardner appeared to be genuinely bewildered at her final claim.

"I may have done a few of those things, but I certainly didn't chop any teddy bears. A guy's gotta be twisted to do something like that! I never did anything like that," Mr. Gardner denied.

"If you didn't, who did?" Jenny countered.

"Beats me," the contractor said.

"I'd like to," Jenny muttered, her hands propped on her hips as she stood there glaring at the trussed-up man.

It turned out that the police officers who responded to her phone call were the same ones who'd shown up last night. "Seems like you two have had some more excitement here tonight," Bert noted as he and his partner entered the studio.

"I caught this guy attacking my wife," Rafe told the police officers. "He was wearing a ski mask and had broken into the studio. He's confessed that he was the one behind the acts of sabotage.''

"But not the bears," Mr. Gardner inserted. "I didn't lay a hand on the bears.''

"Then what were you doing in here tonight?" Jenny demanded.

"I was supposed to spray paint a few of the bears...."

Rafe held Jenny back as she looked ready to do Gardner bodily harm.

"But that's not the same as breaking their arms," the contractor maintained. "That's much worse. You accused me of breaking their arms and chopping them up, and I never did any such—"

"Come on." The police officers helped Gardner to his feet and began reading him his rights as they replaced the extension cord with a pair of handcuffs.

As the officers led Gardner out, Jenny heard Bert say to him, "Hey, weren't you the contractor that put that screened porch in on my house last spring? I *thought* you looked familiar. Well, buddy, the thing's already falling apart...."

"You know what this means, don't you?" Rafe said once the police had taken Gardner away. "That the weirdo who chopped up your bears may still be out there."

"Maybe Mr. Gardner was lying. It doesn't make sense for MegaToys to have paid off two people to harass me," Jenny pointed out.

"It doesn't make sense for them to have paid off *one*, and they're going to pay for it."

"They already are," Jenny said. "I heard on the late news tonight that MegaToys was involved in a huge buyout scheme that went wrong and they're being investigated by the authorities for alleged improprieties. I should think they'll have bigger problems to deal with than me or my bear company for some time to come now.''

"And what if Gardner wasn't the one who broke in here last night?" Rafe demanded.

"If you're trying to scare me, you're succeeding," she shakily assured him.

"I'm not trying to scare you. Do you have any idea how I felt finding that you'd left the house without telling me? And then walking in here and finding you fighting off that goon." He reached out to cup her cheek with his hand, as if needing to physically reassure himself of her well-being. "You could have been badly hurt here tonight."

"I realize that. I didn't plan on coming over here," she earnestly assured him. "I was just going to go for a quick walk around your place. And then since I was so close, I thought I'd pick up some work to do tonight as it didn't look like I was going to get much sleep anyway...." Her voice trailed away as she saw the look on his face. Sighing, she said, "Just do me a favor, Rafe, and don't yell at me or lecture me. I've already had enough excitement for one day, okay?"

She sounded so weary and discouraged that Rafe didn't have the heart to ball her out for being on her own. She already knew she'd made a mistake. There was no point rubbing her nose in it. For the time being, he was just thankful she was unharmed.

So instead of playing the lecturing husband, he simply helped her lock up and fussed over her as he had that night when her roof had leaked and the studio had flooded. Then, as now, he wanted to protect her. To keep her safe. He practically supervised her getting into her pajamas before tucking her into bed.

Jenny hesitated, unsure how to treat this new Rafe. Was he just "being nice" to her, as he'd done when she'd cried on her honeymoon night? Or was it something more?

Sensing her hesitation, Rafe attributed it to delayed trauma as a result of her being attacked. He was determined not to push her. Only a complete heel would take advantage of a woman under these circumstances. So he tried to reassure her, by keeping his touch and his voice warm but not sensual as he'd helped her into bed. After donning a pair of pajama bottoms, he joined her there.

Only when she'd finally fallen asleep did Rafe push the featherbed "bundling board" out of his way and gather her in his arms. Mumbling in her sleep, she shifted against him until she got comfortable in her new position before settling down again.

Rafe found it much more difficult to get any shut-eye as the prospect of almost having lost Jenny resurrected old fears and old wounds still not completely healed.

By the time Jenny woke up and was coherent enough to aim a look at the bedside alarm clock, she realized it was almost eleven in the morning. Rafe must have turned off the alarm. Then she remembered that today was Saturday and she didn't have to open her studio.

She stretched, unable to believe it was really that late. Only then did she realize that the rolled-up featherbed was in a pile at the foot of the bed. She frowned, wondering if her memories of being held safe and secure all night had been dreams or reality.

Rafe had left her a note on the bedside table.

Rest up this morning. Sleep as long as you can. Pop took Cindy to the library for story time this morning, so enjoy the peace and quiet while you can.

Rafe

It was the first time she'd ever seen his writing, aside from his signature on the marriage certificate. She studied the scrawled lines closely, as if searching for the secret to his soul. Tracing her fingers around the bold curve of his *Rs*, she decided his writing reflected his passion and his impatience.

She'd almost carried his note to her breast, to hold it against her heart, when she caught herself. She was acting like a lovesick schoolgirl here, getting her first note from her boyfriend in study hall.

The ring of the phone was a welcome interruption and she grabbed the receiver off the hook.

"*Oy vey*, what's this I hear about you getting attacked last night?" Miriam demanded. "Are you all right? Did they catch the *goniff?*"

"I'm fine and they caught him. It was Mr. Gardner."

"The shyster contractor? I should have known. I never had a good feeling about him. It was his eyes. He had shifty eyes. What about the bears? Did he hurt any of them?"

"No. And he claims he wasn't the one who broke in the other night. Said he'd never chop up a teddy bear, although he had brought a can of spray paint along with him last night to use on my bears."

Jenny didn't have to know Yiddish to know that Miriam was swearing a blue streak. Once she'd calmed down, Miriam said, "Do you believe him, about not chopping up the bears?"

"I don't know," Jenny confessed.

"I don't like this, Jenny."

"I'm not wild about it myself, Miriam," she dryly retorted.

"What does Rafe say?"

"Not much. He was actually very nice. He didn't even ball me out for going over to the studio last night."

"Does he think that *goniff* Gardner is telling the truth?"

"He thinks there's a good possibility that the 'weirdo,' as he put it, is still at large."

"So what good is a security system?" Miriam demanded.

"I'm afraid that's partially my fault," Jenny admitted. "I used my birthdate as the code to undo the alarm system. It wasn't that difficult for Mr. Gardner to find out what day I was born and then try punching it in. It worked."

"I thought you changed the code."

"I did. I used my name before. Not a good idea, either. I know that now. Rafe gave me a minilecture about it last night when he put me to bed. I can assure you that next time I'll be using a password that won't be so easy for someone else to figure out."

"Rafe put you to bed? Sounds like you got something good out of the evening after all," Miriam noted.

"He was just being nice."

"Sure. And Mount Washington is just a little anthill," Miriam mockingly retorted. "You and Rafe aren't still having problems, are you? You can tell me I'm being nosy and should mind my own business—"

"You're being nosy and should mind your own business," Jenny said affectionately, knowing Miriam would pay her no heed.

"But I say you should stop already with all this angst and just follow your heart."

After hanging up a short time later, Jenny noted that Miriam's advice might sound good but things weren't that simple. While Rafe had seemed genuinely concerned about her last night, and relieved that she was okay, he'd treated her like a sister as he'd put her to bed last night. Was that the behavior of a man in love? How should she know? She'd never had a man in love with her before, so she was certainly no expert. In fact, she was working completely in the dark here.

When Rafe had first come into the studio last night, tugging her into his arms after subduing Mr. Gardner, she'd sensed something different in his embrace. A new level of emotion. Could it have been love?

Jenny didn't know. But she *did* know that she couldn't sit up here brooding about it all day. Half the day was gone already.

By the time she took a shower and washed her hair, it was almost noon. To boost her spirits, she decided to wear a tunic-length, bright cherry-red plush velour top with snaps down the front. She teamed it with a pair of black stirrup pants. Before going downstairs, she took Rafe's note and slid it into the back compartment of her suitcase in the closet, right next to the blue topaz pendant he'd given her as a wedding present.

She stopped to grab a cup of coffee in the small kitchen of their private quarters on her way down to the ground floor. Jenny entered the restaurant's kitchen area just as Chuck and Cindy were coming in from their morning at the library.

"And after that the dragon blew fire and the mouse had to run away and hide or get burnt up," Cindy was saying. "Daddy, are you listening to me?"

"Of course I am," Rafe replied, albeit rather absently. "I always listen to you."

"Okay. And after that, the mouse... Wait, I lost my place. Where was I?"

"You were telling me about the story you heard at the library."

"We didn't just hear it, Daddy. We watched it, too. They had a real storyteller there and she had puppets for the mouse and the dragon. It was so impressive!"

"Sounds like it. You can tell me the rest later. You better go wash up for lunch, kiddo."

Cindy did as he asked. Looking up and seeing Jenny hovering on the threshold, Rafe said, "There you are. Just in time. Hugo has been preparing something special for us."

"What's the occasion?" Jenny asked.

"Capturing the no-good scum who broke into your place," Spud replied.

"Yeah, but another no-good scum may still be out there," Rafe noted broodingly. "Gardner claims he never chopped up those teddy bears. Claims it must have been done by a pervert."

"Do not speak of such things in my kitchen," Hugo declared with an agitated wave of his spoon, nearly splattering Rafe with the stew gravy.

"What kind of lowlife would chop the arms off a teddy bear?" Spud demanded.

"I don't know." Jenny shook her head. "But when they find this guy, I'm going to break *his* arms and see how he likes it!" she declared, the light of battle in her eyes.

"You'll have to stand in line," Rafe retorted, having moved out of Hugo's spoon range. "I get first shot at the guy."

Out of the corner of her eye, Jenny noticed that Hugo was now stirring his pot with so much overwrought energy that the gravy was sloshing over the side and getting onto the burner.

"You break his arms and I'll break his legs," Chuck declared.

"I'm with you, buddy," Spud agreed. "Hey, what's the matter, Hughie? You're looking a little green around the edges there."

"All this talk of violence is not good for someone of my sensitive disposition," Hugo informed them, clearly flustered by their discussion.

Once Cindy returned from the bathroom, the conversation moved on to another subject as Rafe and his family headed for the dining room table. Jenny was surprised to note that Rafe held out the chair for her. The old-world courtesy touched her.

Hugo, his face still flushed from his earlier agitation, brought his specialty hearty stew-soup and set it on the table with a flourish. "Pot-au-feu with artichokes."

"Pot of fire," Spud translated. "Looks like you almost burnt it this time. You must have been really upset by all our talk to have overcooked your stew this way, Hughie. Now don't you go having a hissy fit about it." Spud thumped him on the shoulder as Hugo appeared ready to have a conniption. "I'll do the serving and you can go back to the kitchen. Wouldn't want you burning anything else."

His face now scarlet, Hugo seemed unable to even sniff his disapproval before making his departure.

"I suppose I shouldn't really pick on him that way," Spud ruefully acknowledge once Hugo had left. "But I don't seem able to help myself. There's just something about the guy... you know? Here, Jenny." He handed her the first plateful of the stew.

Jenny took the plate and set it down in front of her. Blinking, she looked at her plate again. "I'm really going off the deep end here," she murmured. "This almost looks like..." She scraped off the onion, carrot and gravy. "It is!" She held up a small teddy bear arm about two inches in length. It was from one of her bears; she recognized the soft honey brown mohair of the unjointed bear that had been ruthlessly chopped up two nights ago. "It's one of the arms from my mutilated bears!"

"Hugo, get in here!" Rafe curtly ordered. Once the chef was standing beside the table, Rafe coldly inquired, "Would you care to explain how that got in your stew?"

"I found it," Cindy piped.

"Where did it come from?" Rafe asked her.

"I found it in Hugo's soilly room."

"The Soleil room." Rafe recognized his daughter's pronunciation of the walk-in closet with windows and a southern exposure that served as Hugo's depository for his cookbook collection. *Soleil*. French for sun.

"I found it there and put it on the kitchen table," Cindy continued.

"And I was distracted. I must not have noticed. It looked like sausage. Yes, that explains it, then," Hugo hurriedly said, about to rush away.

"No, it doesn't. What was one of Jenny's teddy-bear arms doing in your Soleil room, Hugo?" Rafe's voice remained icy.

Like a sand castle hit with a big wave, Hugo just seemed to crumble. "I did it for the kitchen," he wailed. "I need a bigger kitchen! I deserve a bigger kitchen and more fame." His eyes glowed with a fanatic fervor. "It's only right. It's only fair. I did what I had to do."

"What exactly did you do, Hugo?" Rafe demanded.

"What had to be done. I was sure that when Jenny married you she would give you the barn. But it didn't work that way. She just wouldn't give up. I realized that someone else was already making trouble. But they were working too slowly. I know she loves those bears, the way I love my solid copper pans from France. So I damaged them. To make her move out of the barn and sell the property to you, Rafe." Hugo turned to give Rafe a look imploring his understanding. "So you could have the extension to the restaurant that you wanted."

"An extension that included a spanking new, huge kitchen for Hugo as well as banquet facilities," Rafe muttered, comprehension dawning.

"That's right." Sinking into an empty chair, Hugo stared off into space and began incoherently babbling, "It was for the kitchen, you see. You can understand that, can't you? It was for the kitchen. For the kitchen."

* * *

"Rafe, we have to talk." It had been hours since the authorities had come and taken Hugo away. Hours that Rafe had spent holed up in his office, which she'd finally located with some help from Chuck.

Closing the door behind her, Jenny couldn't fail to notice how cold and withdrawn Rafe was acting. She wondered if he blamed her for all the trouble—her refusal to sell the land to him had apparently driven Hugo off the deep end, and now Rafe had to find another chef. Jenny knew that whatever else he might be, Hugo had been an outstanding chef and an invaluable asset to Rafe's restaurant. And now he was gone.

"Don't you think we should talk about this?" she said.

"No." His expression was as distant as his voice.

"Well, I do." But Jenny found it very difficult to talk about what had happened when Rafe refused to participate in any kind of two-way dialogue. In no time at all, his brooding silence drove her up a wall.

"Are you going to just sit there like some kind of sphinx made out of stone?" she ended up yelling at him.

"I'm not made out of stone!" Rafe yelled back.

"Finally, some kind of response," she noted with approval. "Does that mean you're ready to tell me how you feel? Why you're acting so cold and distant? I realize Hugo was a valuable asset to your restaurant and that you're upset because you've lost him—"

"You don't understand anything," Rafe angrily inserted.

"Fine, then," she shot back. "Why don't you explain it to me?"

"I feel to blame for what happened."

"You? What on earth for?"

"Because Hugo worked for me. I should have seen some sign that my chef was going off the deep end. I always con-

sidered Hugo to be high-strung, but I never realized he was
capable of doing anything like this. You could have been
hurt as a result of my failure to recognize Hugo's instabil-
ity. What if Hugo had come after you instead of your teddy
bears?''

So that was it. ''Anyone ever tell you that you've got an
overdeveloped sense of responsibility?''

''Yeah, it might have been mentioned to me one or two
times,'' Rafe muttered. In fact, Susan had told him that
when she was very sick. Quietly told him it wasn't his fault
she had gotten leukemia and told him he shouldn't blame
himself. At the time he'd thought Susan had just been saying that to make him feel better. But Jenny wasn't like Susan. She didn't tell him what he wanted to hear. She told him
the truth. Straight-out, no-holds-barred.

Placing her hands on his desk the same way he'd once
done with her, Jenny leaned forward and stared him straight
in the eye. ''No one, other than Hugo himself, is to blame
for what happened,'' she clearly enunciated. ''Except perhaps for that friend of Hugo's from the South Bronx who
helped him bypass the security system. But I certainly don't
hold you responsible. I mean you could just as well have
said that this was all my fault for setting off the whole thing
in the first place by not selling out to you when you offered
to buy my property.''

''Don't be ridiculous.''

''I won't if you won't.''

He returned her direct gaze and Jenny stared into his dark
blue eyes, wishing she could decipher the depth of emotion
hidden there.

They were interrupted by a knock on the door. ''Sorry to
butt in here,'' Chuck said. ''But Cindy is waiting upstairs
for you two to tuck her in.''

Jenny had taken Cindy upstairs right after Hugo's
breakdown, so the little girl hadn't known about the au-

thorities coming to get him. Since Hugo had been known to weep over a soufflé gone wrong, the sight of the high-strung chef in tears hadn't upset Cindy as much is it might have done otherwise.

The little girl was waiting for them, for once without the *Sleeping Beauty* book in her hands.

"Know where babies come from?" she asked them. "I do. Grandpa got me the book from the li-bary today." She held it up for them to see. "I wanna baby sister for my birthday, okay?"

Rafe and Jenny looked at each other uncertainly.

"Don't you know how to have babies?" Cindy demanded. "Daddy, you didn't forget how, did you? I was a baby once, remember?"

"Yeah, and you were a lot quieter then," Rafe muttered, a wave of red staining his high cheekbones.

"You know the mommy and daddy have to love each other. Don' you guys love each other?" Cindy demanded, her questioning techniques once again putting the Spanish Inquisition to shame, just as they had the first day Jenny had moved to North Dunway. "Well, you do, don' you?"

Rafe nodded.

Taking her cue from him, so did Jenny, although she suspected she was the only one telling the truth here.

"Good," Cindy said, clearly well pleased. "Don' forget. A baby sister. If he's a boy, you gotta take him back," Cindy cheerfully informed them.

Once they'd finally gotten her settled for the night and had left her room, Jenny caught up with Rafe in the living room. "I realize you were only agreeing to make her happy...."

"I do love you," Rafe huskily admitted. "I want this to be a real marriage."

Jenny couldn't have been more stunned had he grown wings and taken flight.

"We've got to let go of the past," he continued. "The bottom line is that both of us have to learn how to trust again. It won't be easy but I think it will be worth it. We just need to learn to trust life again. We've both been kicked in the teeth. But that doesn't mean that we have to throw in the towel. Maybe we should try looking at this thing another way."

"What do you mean?"

"That we've already endured the suffering first and now it's time for the happiness. That we deserve to be happy. That we weren't to blame for what happened in our past. Neither one of us, Jenny," he said.

"I always thought it was me," Jenny admitted in a whisper. "That my father left because of me."

"And I thought that Susan died because of me."

"But she died of leukemia, Rafe. There was nothing you could do."

"And there was nothing you could have done either to make your father stay. He was a selfish jerk. Otherwise he would never have left you. It was never about you, don't you see? It was him. All him."

The tears were flowing down Jenny's cheeks and she didn't realize until that moment how much she'd needed to hear what Rafe had just said. That it wasn't her fault. Which meant that maybe she was lovable after all.

Reaching out to wipe away her tears, Rafe said, "Instead of being afraid because life has kicked us in the teeth, we could decide that we've been zapped already and that the worst is over with now. That only better things are ahead for us. What do you say?"

"I say that I love you, Rafe Murphy."

"I'm so glad, Mrs. Murphy."

His grin was a sight to behold, Jenny noted mistily.

Taking her by the hand, he said, "Come on, let's go."

"Where?"

"To start our honeymoon. I'd say it's long overdue, wouldn't you?"

Jenny nodded her agreement.

Once they were upstairs, Rafe picked her up, sweeping her off her feet instead of tossing her over his shoulder as he had once before. "What are you doing?" she asked.

"Carrying you over the threshold. We're going to do this right," he told her as he carefully set her down on the bed.

"You mean the full honeymoon treatment?" Jenny inquired with a grin.

"Definitely the full treatment. But first, we get rid of this thing...." He tossed the bundling board-cum-featherbed onto the floor. "And then we get rid of this...." Reaching out, he unsnapped her velour top, one snap at a time, making the excitement and the anticipation all the greater by his protracted deliberation.

"Then I suppose this should go, too," she murmured, obligingly undoing the buttons on his shirt.

Their arms became tangled in the interim and they ended up laughing before Rafe leaned down to kiss her. Jenny tugged him with her as she fell back onto the bed.

His kiss was as passionate as ever but it was now laced with rich emotion, freely expressing his love for her with every stroke of his hand, and every nuance of his tongue. To Jenny it was like tasting chocolate after years of abstinence, only better. Actually there was nothing in her life that could compare to this. She'd thought the passion between them couldn't get any better. She was wrong. Being able to show her love, trusting that he'd be there for her to love, knowing that he loved her in return, it made all the difference in the world.

And then he murmured her name, telling her how much he loved her, whispering lusty promises of things to come. Removing her already-opened top, he placed a necklace of kisses around her collarbone as he undid her bra. "You're beautiful," he said huskily. "The first time I saw you, I thought—"

"That I was a crazy woman attacking you with a teddy bear," she inserted wryly.

"No." He kissed her as sweet punishment for her words. "I thought that you were a Venus in blue jeans."

"You did?"

Rafe nodded. "But instead of talking about how I feel, why don't I just show you...?" Leaning down, he bathed her breasts with kisses, showering her with caresses—from the lightest brush of his hand as he just skimmed a rosy crest to cupping her in his palm and surrounding her with his touch.

Unlike the rushed passion of their previous embraces, this time he took his time—as if aware that there was no need to hurry, that they had the rest of their lives to savor a curve of an arm, or the shape of a mouth or the shell of an ear. Jenny reciprocated in kind, lingering over the shadowy outline of his jaw, extending the sensual declaration of his kiss as his mouth returned to possess her parted lips.

The buildup was prolonged, the pleasure was equally so as they shed the remainder of their clothing and made love. With every stroke of his hand, Rafe took her to a new level of delight, so that when he finally came to her she welcomed him with a cry of satisfaction. His movements filled her with joy, setting off a chain reaction that washed over her—wave after wave—originating deep within her and rippling out to every corner of her body as she clenched him to her, holding on to him as the surge of motion propelled her from this world into another.

Steeped in satisfaction and basking in the resultant afterglow of their lovemaking, Jenny lay with her face nestled in the hollow of Rafe's throat. She pressed her lips against his pulse, monitoring its eventual slowing from the racing thrum of lingering passion to the steady beat of fulfillment.

"You know, I never did give you a wedding present," Jenny noted in a soft voice.

Rafe tipped her face up to his so that he could see her. "What we just shared was present enough," he assured her with a wolfish grin.

"I'm serious."

"So am I," he told her with a devilish gleam in his eye.

She put her hand out to stop him from kissing her and distracting her. "I want to give you the house as my wedding present. That way you should still be able to expand Murphy's. After all, I really bought the property for the barn and not the house. If we put the access drive to my studio on the far side of the lot, I'm sure an architect could come up with a creative way of combining the two houses into one building."

"Jenny, I can't accept—"

She placed her fingers over his lips. "Shh. Consider it a present for our children."

"Our children, huh? I like the sound of that," he noted with a possessive gleam in his eyes.

"I do, too." Placing his hand on her stomach she said, "Just one more thing. Contrary to what Cindy thinks, if the baby is a boy, we're keeping him."

"And I'm keeping you . . . close to my heart," Rafe whispered, kissing her softly. "Always. Now do you have anything else you'd like to say before we begin work on creating those children?"

"Well, now that you mention it, this room could use some work," she noted, with a meaningful look over his shoulder. "A dresser for me, a few chairs, perhaps some pictures on the walls. I have some watercolors that would look great with the blue rug. And Bruiser would look great on top of your dresser," she added, warmed by the knowledge that finally Rafe's house felt like home and that she felt as if she belonged.

"I don't think Bruiser is old enough to view what I have in store for you," Rafe murmured.

"No?" Jenny asked with a sexy grin.

"No," he assured her before showing her yet again how much he loved her and always would.

*   *   *   *   *

Dark secrets, dangerous desire...

Lovers DARK AND DANGEROUS

Three spine-tingling tales from the dark side of love.

This October, enter the world of shadowy romance as Silhouette presents the third in their annual tradition of thrilling love stories and chilling story lines. Written by three of Silhouette's top names:

LINDSAY McKENNA
LEE KARR
RACHEL LEE

Haunting a store near you this October.

MILLION DOLLAR SWEEPSTAKES (III)

SWP-S994

The Loop ™

Is the future what it's cracked up to be?

This September, tune in to see why Jessica's partying days are over in

GETTING IT RIGHT: JESSICA
by Carla Cassidy

She had flunked out of college and nearly out of life. Her father expected her to come crawling home, and her friends expected her to fall off the wagon…but Jessica decided she'd rather sell her soul before she screwed up again. So she squeezed into an apartment with some girls she barely knew, got a job that barely paid the bills and decided that things were looking up. Trouble was, no one knew better than her that _looks_ could be deceiving.

The ups and downs of modern life continue with

GETTING REAL: CHRISTOPHER
by Kathryn Jensen in October

GETTING PERSONAL: BECKY
by Janet Quin Harkin in November

Get smart. Get into "The Loop!"

Only from

Silhouette® ™

where passion lives.

LOOP2

JINGLE BELLS, WEDDING BELLS:
Silhouette's Christmas Collection for 1994

Christmas Wish List

*To beat the crowds at the malls and get the perfect present for *everyone,* even that snoopy Mrs. Smith next door!

*To get through the holiday parties without running my panty hose.

*To bake cookies, decorate the house and serve the perfect Christmas dinner—just like the women in all those magazines.

*To sit down, curl up and read my Silhouette Christmas stories!

Join *New York Times* bestselling author Nora Roberts, along with popular writers Barbara Boswell, Myrna Temte and Elizabeth August, as we celebrate the joys of Christmas—and the magic of marriage—with

JINGLE BELLS, WEDDING BELLS

Silhouette's Christmas Collection for 1994.

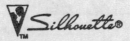

Jilted!

Left at the altar, but not for long.

Why are these six couples
who have sworn off love
suddenly hearing wedding bells?

Find out in these scintillating books
by your favorite authors,
coming this November!

#889   **THE ACCIDENTAL BRIDEGROOM**
by Ann Major
(Man of the Month)

#890   **TWO HEARTS, SLIGHTLY USED**
by Dixie Browning

#891   **THE BRIDE SAYS NO**
by Cait London

#892   **SORRY, THE BRIDE HAS ESCAPED**
by Raye Morgan

#893   **A GROOM FOR RED RIDING HOOD**
by Jennifer Greene

#894   **BRIDAL BLUES**
by Cathie Linz

Come join the festivities when six handsome
hunks finally walk down the aisle...

only from

SILHOUETTE® Desire®

JILT

ANNETTE BROADRICK'S
SONS OF TEXAS
SERIES CONTINUES

Available in October from Silhouette Desire,
TEMPTATION TEXAS STYLE! (SD #883) is the latest
addition to Annette Broadrick's series about the
Callaway family.

Roughed-up rodeo cowboy Tony Callaway thought
women were nothing but trouble—but once this
lonesome cowboy took one look into Christina
O'Reilly's sultry green eyes, he was sure to change
his mind!

Don't miss Tony Callaway's story in TEMPTATION
TEXAS STYLE! by Annette Broadrick, Desire's MAN OF
THE MONTH for October.

He's one of the SONS OF TEXAS and
ready to ride into your heart!